MCCRACKEN
AND THE
LOST VALLEY

By Mark Adderley

Yankton, South Dakota

2013

D1711632

Published by Scriptorium Press,
Yankton, South Dakota

To Father Dave Erickson
and Father James (Jamie) Walling

Contents

I had arrived at Chateau Jaubert, the ancestral home of my good friend Nicolas Jaubert, too late to see anything of its ancient lines. All I could see was the square of yellow light flooding from a ground-floor window. Fritz, my servant and chauffeur, stopped the silver Daimler in front of the steps that led to the magnificent front door, and waited while I rang the bell. The chimes sounded deep within the chateau, rather like the bells that tolled regularly on ships, and I was reminded of Jaubert's fascination with the sea—with everything that floated upon it or swam in it.

After a moment's pause, the door opened, and a man dressed in what looked like eighteenth-century livery, with buckled shoes, tails, and even a powdered wig, stood framed in the light.

"Monsieur McCracken?" he inquired, in slow, measured tones.

"I am," I said.

"Monsieur Jaubert is expecting you; follow me, *s'il vous plâit.*" Peering past my shoulder almost surreptitiously, he added, "Monsieur's man may take the motor-car to the side of the house."

I looked back and signaled to Fritz, who nodded and put the Daimler into gear. The car purred away round the corner as I entered the house, the butler shutting the door softly behind me. I found myself in a long hall, dominated by a large crucifix, with doors on either side and a great stone staircase directly ahead of me. Shields bearing a variety of devices hung on the walls, and suits of armour flanked the staircase. Overhead hung the huge iron wheel of a candelabrum. The butler led me into one of the rooms off to the right, full of books and leather-backed chairs and a leaping fire that looked most welcoming. As we entered, Jaubert, a wiry man a few inches shorter and a few years older than I, unfolded himself from one of the chairs nearest the fire and, setting aside his book, embraced me and kissed me on either cheek in the French fashion.

"McCracken!" he cried. "It is *très merveilleux* to see you! Welcome to my home!" He turned to the butler. "Albert," he said, "see to it that Monsieur McCracken's luggage is taken up to his room." Turning back to me, he asked, "Are you hungry, my friend?" I shook my head, and he said to Albert, "At once, Albert."

"*Tout de suite, monsieur,*" replied Albert, and left us.

Jaubert poured us each a Cognac and we sat opposite one another beside the fire. As we sipped appreciatively, he asked, "And how is Madame McCracken?"

Jaubert and I had not seen each other since my wedding, six months previously. "Delightful, as always," I replied. "I find I can't get away with anything now. She's currently in Scotland, doing some research in the special collection of medieval manuscripts at the University of St. Andrews."

"Ah, *quel dommage*!" lamented Jaubert with a sigh. "I had so much wanted to see her again."

For a while, we reminisced about what we had been doing since the rather dangerous adventure we had shared in Greece last summer. In time, though, our conversation turned—inevitably, as it was September 1914—to politics and war.

"*Oui*, McCracken," said Jaubert, shaking his head sadly, "I fear that very soon my beloved France will be overrun by the Boche; already, he is in Belgium."

"But so is your army, and the British Expeditionary Force," I reminded him. "All is not lost." I took a sip of Cognac. "You and I knew this would happen, a year ago. If our governments had done as we advised, it could have been avoided."

"It is always a mistake to get involved in politics," answered Jaubert.

Partly to divert him from his melancholy mood, I asked, "Have you heard anything from Sikorsky lately?"

"Ah, *oui*," replied Jaubert. "I heard from him not three weeks ago. He is in health, and wishes you to know that he still works on the airship, which he hopes will be operational within a month."

Shortly after this, we bade each other a good night, and Albert showed me to my room.

The next morning, after Mass, Jaubert showed me around the chateau. His family had held it since the fourteenth century, he explained; like other noble families, the Jauberts had fallen on hard times following the Revolution, but they had managed to retain most of their land. They had done this, Jaubert explained as he led me up on the wall-walks, because they had never behaved tyrannically towards their tenants. "Philippe Jaubert, Marquis de Devizh, always allowed his tenants to run things their own way, and took only minimal rents." He waved a hand at the early nineteenth-century wing below us. "This modern wing," he said, "was built by the tenants to express their love and admiration for Philippe. Their loyalty was such that they would not allow Bonaparte's men to steal from the estate—not much, anyway."

I leaned out on the thick stone wall. The medieval tower was off to our left, now punctuated with modern windows rather than arrow-slits. Below us were the gardens—trees laid out in straight, almost mechanical lines, turning to brass for autumn, square blocks of flower beds, now dark with the lateness of the year, and off to the south the hint of a rocky coast and pounding waves.

"You do not see the gardens at their best, McCracken," Jaubert assured me. "Now, the colours are those of autumn, but in the summer—red, gold, blue, white. It is like heraldry."

"It looks like you have a visitor," I said, pointing: a motor-car approached along the gravel driveway. It was a black saloon, a Brasier Beline, last year's model—3.2 litre, four cylinders, sixteen horsepower, a real beauty with its polished coachwork and the burnished lamps on either side of the driver's seat.

"Hm," commented Jaubert. "I wonder who it could be?"

"He must be wealthy," I said, as we returned to the library. "That's not a cheap motor-car."

Albert had set up coffee in the library, and Jaubert poured me one. I was just adding the cream, when Albert entered, announcing, "*Monsieur Alexandre Millerand désire vous voir, monsieur.*"

Jaubert's eyes sprang open—I hadn't seen him more surprised, even when an ancient civilization had emerged from the Mediterranean last summer. "Show him in at once, Albert," he said. To me, he added, "Monsieur Millerand is the French Minister of War!"

Millerand was a sprightly man in his fifties, with tousled grey hair, a bushy moustache, and round spectacles. The unkempt hair was an odd contrast with the neatly-pressed and expensive suit he wore. He entered the room with punctiliousness, shook Jaubert's hand, and then mine, and began talking rapidly in French.

"Monsieur Millerand, with respect, may we please speak English before my guest?"

"That depends very much, Monsieur Jaubert, on the identity of your guest."

"I'm McCracken," I said.

Millerand's eyebrows rose half an inch. "The famous Scottish engineer?" he asked.

"The Scottish engineer, at any rate," I replied.

"But this is *fantastique!*" exclaimed Millerand. "Monsieur Jaubert, I am here to ask you where I can find Monsieur McCracken, and here he is at your house!"

"*Quel fortune, Monsieur Millerand!*" replied Jaubert.

Millerand nodded in agreement, then placed his attaché case on the desk, flipped it open and took out a piece of fabric, bluish-white in colour, and covered with strange symbols, like a foreign alphabet. He spread it out on the desk. "Monsieur McCracken, the French government needs very urgently your help," he said.

Jaubert and I joined him, peering down at the strange manuscript. Millerand went on, "It is your reputation as a man of science, Monsieur McCracken, which has guided our choice. Professor Jolicoleur of the École Polytechnique recommended you, recalling a paper you delivered at the Royal Academy some years ago."

"I'm flattered," I said. "I remember him well, but didn't think he'd remember me. I studied Chemistry at Imperial, though mechanical engineering was always my strong suit." I indicated the manuscript. "What do we have here?" I asked.

"We had hoped that you could tell us that, monsieur."

"How did you obtain it?" I asked. "And what are its properties?"

"Please allow me to answer your second question first, monsieur," said Millerand and, plucking the fabric from the desk, he flung it into the fire. Jaubert and I cried out, but after a few seconds, it became evident that the thing did not burn.

I looked at Millerand questioningly. "Asbestos?" I guessed.

"At first, we thought so too, monsieur," he replied. "As you know, asbestos has recently become associated with certain diseases of the lung, and it would be a very great benefit if we could develop a flame-retardant fabric that could replace it. But this is not asbestos." He took a pair of tongs from beside the fire, and drew the fabric out. I took it from him. It was warm to the touch, but cooled rapidly as I held it.

"It feels soft," I said. "Almost as soft as silk."

"It has one more property, monsieur," said Millerand, "but we will have to take it outside to demonstrate it. And we will need a firearm. Monsieur Jaubert?"

"*D'accord*," replied Jaubert.

A few moments later, we were on the lawn at the back of the chateau, Millerand holding the manuscript as if it were a pocket handkerchief. I expected him to sniff delicately into it at any moment. After a short time, the door opened again, and Jaubert strode towards us, a revolver in his hand, slipping a round into the chamber. He handed the gun to the minister.

"*Merci beaucoup*," said Millerand. He placed the manuscript on the ground, took a couple of steps back, and fired the gun.

The shot echoed for a few seconds, and a whiff of cordite hung upon the air. A few crows croaked in surprise from the nearby trees. There was a hole in the lawn, and the edges of the fabric showed above it. I bent down, twisted the manuscript around my fingers, and pulled. It was lodged fast, but when I wriggled it a little, it eased out. Something heavy hung inside it, and I wondered for a moment how a pebble could have got into it. It seemed to have no hole in it at all. Mystified, I unfolded it, and we saw what was inside: it was the spent bullet.

"Great Scott!" I exclaimed.

"*Sacré Bleu!*" exclaimed Jaubert.

"You see, *messieurs*?" said Millerand. "A fabric that is flame-retardant and bullet-proof as well!" He took the fabric back, handed the revolver to Jaubert (who began to unload it instantly), and together we strolled back towards the chateau. Millerand went on, "As you know, *messieurs*, war has just broken out in Europe. Such a fabric, if used in German uniforms, could tip the balance of power on the Western Front."

"The bullet didn't pierce the fabric," I pointed out, "but that would still have killed the wearer."

"Perhaps," answered Millerand, "or perhaps not, if the layers of fabric are doubled. Who can tell? But think of it—if the Germans were to weave enough of this fabric and use it to construct Zeppelins, then their ultimate weapons would be unstoppable."

We were back in the library by now, and I asked, "Where did you get this stuff, Mr. Millerand?"

"That is partially what gives us such a cause for alarm," replied Millerand. "Let me begin the story, as I know it, at the beginning, rather than at the point where I came in.

"As you know, the Germans invaded Belgium several weeks ago, in an attempt to seize Paris, so that they could then turn their attention to their eastern enemies, the Russians. I believe the conquest of Belgium took longer than they expected, however, and resistance to occupation was fierce. As a reprisal for acts of violence against German occupying forces, and to deter further resistance, the Germans set fire to the city of Leuven. One of the buildings they destroyed was the library of the Catholic University of Leuven."

"I heard about that," I said. "A tragedy."

"Indeed, *monsieur*," replied Millerand. "These Boches, they are uncultured animals. But to resume. A few days later, a private in the German army, picking his way through the wreckage, discovered a piece of fabric, showing no signs of burning. It was not in the records of the university at all."

"No, but scraps of fabric were often used to stiffen up the binding of books in the Middle Ages," I said. "If the cover and the leaves were completely burned away, this piece of fabric might have survived."

Millerand nodded appreciatively. "I did not know that you were an expert on paleography, Monsieur McCracken."

I cleared my throat. "I'm not," I admitted, "but I know someone who is."

Jaubert laughed, delighted. "Monsieur McCracken refers, I think, to his most delightful wife, Madame Ariadne McCracken."

Millerand raised his eyebrows. "She who was Ariadne Bell, related to the American telegraph company's owners?" Jaubert and I both nodded. "My congratulations, monsieur," Millerand said. "If report is accurate, Madame McCracken is indeed a most beautiful woman."

"Report is accurate," I confirmed with pleasure.

"Well, in any case, you have perhaps explained how the fabric got where it did. In any event, this private, a man named Hister or Hilter, took the fabric to his superiors, who were so impressed that they promoted him to corporal on the spot. They sent the fabric away to Munich for analysis, but one of the laboratory assistant, a Dane who was opposed to the German aggression in the current war, cut the manuscript down the middle and took half of it to his home in Copenhagen, where he passed it on to the French ambassador, who sent it in his turn to Paris in the diplomatic bag. Now we bring it to you, Monsieur McCracken, to tell us what you can of it—can the Germans manufacture this? If not, where can they obtain more? And can we obtain it first? The course of the war may very much depend on you, Monsieur McCracken."

CHAPTER 2
THE MYSTERIOUS MANUSCRIPT

I spent the rest of that day examining the strange manuscript. Fortunately, Jaubert had a fair to middling laboratory in the medieval wing of his chateau. It seemed as if I'd been working for only a few minutes when I noticed that I could see almost nothing, that the lab was reduced to shades of blue all around me. I got up, stretched, and lit the gas-lights over the fireplace and another at the desk where I was working.

Someone knocked at the door, and Jaubert entered. "McCracken!" he exclaimed, as if he hadn't seen me in years. "Do you make progress?"

I leaned back in my chair, and held up a metal dish in which was a tiny fragment of the fabric from which the manuscript was made. I explained, "The problem is that most tests you can conduct to identify fabrics are what are called burn tests. The ash of cotton is soft and fine; when you touch it, it turns to dust. Wool becomes black and brittle when burned—you can crush it between your thumb and finger. But of course this stuff is flame-retardant. Honestly, I was surprised I could cut it. Is Millerand still here?"

"No, he had to go back to Paris."

"Well, I'll keep conducting tests, of course, but I think the secret is in these strange symbols."

Jaubert gave a kind of twisted smile. "I think I know who can help us," he said.

"I'll cable her in the morning," I said.

"*Pardonnez-moi, monsieur,*" replied Jaubert, "but I have already taken that liberty—I hope you do not object."

"It'll take a lot to wrench her away from all her medieval manuscripts," I said, "but this might do it, all right."

"In any case," said Jaubert, turning towards the door, "Albert has set the table for dinner. There is but you and I, *mon ami,* so there is no need for formal dress."

I spent most of the next day in the laboratory as well, and when I went to supper (dressed formally, this time, on Jaubert's advice), I found that Fr. Jean-Marie, who celebrated Mass in the chapel, had joined us. Albert stood to attention at Jaubert's shoulder, and we all made the sign of the cross.

"*Bénissez-nous, Seigneur, bénissez ce repas, ceux qui l'ont préparé, et procurez du pain à ceaux qui n'en pas. Ainsi soit-il. Amen.*"

We shook out our serviettes and began the meal. There were tender asparagus tips in hollandaise sauce, mushrooms fried in butter with a hint of garlic, sautéed trout with raspberry vinegar sauce, tarragon, parsley, and green onions. We ate appreciatively in silence for a few minutes, sipping from glasses of white wine (the bottle bore Jaubert's family label), until Jaubert asked, "Can you tell us, McCracken, what you have discovered about the manuscript?"

Fr. Jean-Marie passed me a plate of dinner rolls, still hot from the oven. When I broke one open, a tiny cloud of steam escaped, and the butter melted on impact. "Well," I said, "I can be fairly certain the Germans can't manufacture it."

"How can you be so certain of this, Monsieur McCracken?" asked Fr. Jean-Marie.

"Well, it's not a man-made fibre," I answered. "Under the microscope, it looks a lot like silk—there are a lot of flat areas on the fibres, which is what gives silk its shiny appearance. Silk doesn't stretch much, but this fabric hardly stretches at all. That would make it a little uncomfortable in clothing."

I paused, and Fr. Jean-Marie said, "Go on, Monsieur McCracken."

"When silkworms exude silk fibres, they cover them with a type of protein called sericin. It's sticky, and it's what enables the strands to stick together. I haven't been able to identify the protein that sticks these fibres together, but not only is it sticky, it's flame-retardant. It's also water-proof—you can barely wet the stuff."

"Can you tell where it was made?" asked Jaubert.

"Only very general things," I admitted. "If I were to hazard a guess, I'd say it was woven by worms of some kind—but quite big worms, as the fibres are very large. Silkworms weave cocoons in which they metamorphose—they change from their juvenile state into an adult state. Probably these worms do the same thing, and have to be protected from pretty serious weather in the meantime. It's almost as if they were made inside a volcano or under the ocean."

"Bravo, McCracken!" cried Jaubert. "But how will you find this fabric? Presumably the Boche are even at this moment attempting to do this."

"I?" I repeated. "Surely you'll come too, Jaubert?" I asked. Albert had cleared away the plates and was serving a dessert called *Croquembouche*, little caramel-glazed cream-puffs, with coffee.

"My regrets, McCracken," answered Jaubert, "but this time I may not. Fr. Jean-Marie and I will leave next week on pilgrimage to Santiago de Compostela. We will be gone for a month. And you, I think, will need to leave long before that."

"Hm. I wonder who else I can get for the team," I said to myself.

At that moment, the doorbell rang. Albert looked back at Jaubert for permission, and then walked out into the hallway. A moment later, he returned, followed by a familiar figure.

"Madame Ariadne McCracken, *messieurs*," Albert announced.

Now, my wife is the most beautiful woman I know. I realize every decent husband thinks so, but the difference is, I'm right, and everyone who claps eyes on Ari acknowledges it. Seeing her now, I thought of our desperate moments of danger together, on the Amazon and on the lost island of Thera. Whether she wore britches and a pith helmet for adventuring, or a long dress the colour of burgundy wine, as now, her clothes were merely the frame for her exquisite beauty. The dress was of the latest fashion, I knew, clinging tight like a jacket over her arms and shoulders, and flowering out from the waist, but she wore it because it suited her figure in a way that the narrow corseted waists and bustles of the last decade would not. As usual, on seeing her, I wondered how I could ever have deserved so beautiful and talented a wife.

The men in the room rose to their feet as if they were parts of a well-oiled machine. I kissed Ari on the cheek, Jaubert and Fr. Jean-Marie kissed her on the hand.

"You've made a quick journey of it, my love," I observed.

"Nicolas' cable was very enticing," she replied. *"Have manuscript in strange language. Come soon. Jaubert."*

"*Sauve mon honneur,*" declared Jaubert, "but it is like—how do you say?—old times to be together again. All these days, we men have lacked beauty, and now it is restored to us!"

"You're very kind, Nicolas," said Ari, with a smile. I pulled out a chair for her, while Albert set a plate and glass before her. "What's going on?" she asked.

"Ah, Madame McCracken!" said Jaubert, rising from his seat. "It is this—*un moment, s'il vous plait.*" He left the room, returning a few moments later with the manuscript. By the time he had finished explaining the situation, Ari had almost finished the trout. She set aside her fork—like many Americans, she didn't use a knife except in an extremity of need—and held the fabric up to the light.

"It looks like a Turkic language, and the script has some similarities with Georgian," she said, "but this is very old. I'm not very familiar with the Turkic languages, except modern Turkish, but I might be able to translate it—I'll go quicker if you have Kutsetsov's *Grammar and Lexicon of the Ancient Turkish Languages* in your library, Nicolas."

"*Quel fortune!*" cried Jaubert again. "I have the very book; but only the second volume, I regret."

"That will do for now," said Ari. "That's the lexicon—I can get by without the grammar for now, and assume it's similar to modern Turkish. Can we send out for Volume One?"

Jaubert looked at Albert, who inclined his head and said, "I shall see to it tomorrow, *madame.*"

Jaubert sat back in his chair and beamed at us all. "Yes, but this is just like the Thera business," he said. "I truly wish I could come with you!"

Ari and I got to work the following morning, but it was a long and frustrating day for me. There was really nothing else I could glean from the physical properties of the fabric, and I was desperate to get out and *do* something. Ari, on the other hand, sequestered herself in our room, surrounded by books (some open and face-down, some with torn pieces of paper marking several different places), jotting things down repeatedly in her notebook.

At last, five o'clock came around, and Ari and I went downstairs to find that Fr. Jean-Marie had once more joined us for dinner. I had to report regretfully that I had nothing further to report on the fabric. They turned expectantly to my wife.

"I've translated some of it, but not all. The Dane who stole it from the Germans cut it downwards, so I have two or three words in a sentence, and then it breaks off. But there's a word that keeps cropping up, and it's a real puzzle."

"What word is that, Madame McCracken?" asked Jaubert.

"Well, I don't think it's translatable. It looks like it might be the name of a person or place, or perhaps even a god. In any case, I can't track down the meaning: *Zun*."

"*Zun*?" I repeated. "That sounds familiar." Light began to dawn upon me. "It's a place," I concluded. "I'm certain of it."

"How do you know, Mac?" asked Ari.

"I had a friend a long time ago, when I was a kid in Aberdeen. He was a priest, and he used to tell us kids stories of a place called Zun. He was a big burly chap with a great bushy beard called Fr. Jamie Erickson. "

"*Ma foi*!" cried Fr. Jean-Marie. "I know this man—he and I attended a retreat together last year."

"*Quel fortune*!" cried Jaubert, and then hastily corrected himself: "What is it I say? Not fortune any longer, *messieurs*—perhaps *providence* is a more accurate term!"

"You know Fr. Jamie?" I said in surprise to Fr. Jean-Marie. "Well, coincidence or Providence, it was fantastic stuff he told us—travelers' tales from the Middle Ages, like the stories Marco Polo or John Mandeville told. That's what we'd say to him when he'd finished one: 'Oh, that's a real Marco Polo, that is.' Only he never seemed really to mind—he just enjoyed telling the stories."

"Can you remember any of the details?" asked Ari.

I struggled with my memory for a moment. "No," I said. "There was a king who had a magic mirror and a sceptre made from a single emerald, and an army of cannibals. I wish I could remember more."

"It seems, monsieur," said Fr. Jean-Marie, "that you must find Fr. Jamie Erickson."

I sighed. "It's been so long since I saw him last. I don't know where he could be."

"When I spoke with him last year," said Fr. Jean-Marie, "he was heading towards Portugal. He wished to see someone called Henrique, apparently a prince of Portugal."

"Impossible!" declared Jaubert. All eyes turned on him. "The exiled king of Portugal, Emmanuel II, was married just one year ago. He has had as yet no children."

"I must have misunderstood him," said Fr. Jean-Marie. "But *certainement, messieurs, madame,* he was on his way to Portugal to meet someone called Henrique."

"We need Vasili on the team," said Ari. "Perhaps he's finished fixing the airship."

"Why don't you go to the Ukraine and see if he's busy, dear?" I said. "I'll go to Portugal and try to track down Fr. Jamie."

"Albert can take you to Saint-Malo tomorrow, McCracken," Jaubert assured me. "From there, you can easily get a steamer for Lisbon."

"Will you be needing Fritz?" Ari asked.

"No, I'll go faster alone. Why don't you take him with you?" Ari nodded. "Well," I concluded, "life's been a bit quiet lately—just a war. It'll be nice to be busy again."

After dinner, I paid a quick visit to Jaubert's library, to see if I could discover anything about a Portuguese prince named Henrique. To my surprise, I found a whole article on someone in the latest edition of *Encyclopaedia Britannica*:

"HENRIQUE OF PORTUGAL, surnamed the 'Navigator' (1394-1460), duke of Viseu, governor of the Algarve, was born at Oporto on the 4th of March 1394. He was the third (or, counting children who died in infancy, the fifth) son of John (Joao) I, the founder of the Aviz dynasty, under whom Portugal, victorious against Castile and against the Moors of Morocco, began to take a prominent place among European nations; his mother was Philippa, daughter of John of Gaunt."

I read on: during a military campaign in North Africa, Henrique had heard of the fabled Land of Prester John and, convinced that by finding it he could open up the trade-route from Europe to India, he sent explorers out to Africa to try to discover it.

"In 1419, Henrique was created governor of the 'kingdom' of Algarve, the southernmost province of Portugal; and his connexion now appears to have begun with what afterwards became known as the 'Infante's Town' (Villa do Infante) at Sagres, close to Cape St. Vincent; where, from 1438, the prince certainly resided for a great part of his later life; and where he died in 1460."

The last part of the article described how, as Grand Master of the Order of Christ, Henrique gathered about him on the windswept promontory of Sagres mathematicians, astronomers, cartographers, shipbuilders, navigators, adventurers, fortune-hunters, pilgrims who had visited remote shrines, Christians and Copts and Arabs, anyone who could tell him something about Prester John's Land.

I remembered now that Fr. Jamie had spoken of this Land of Prester John. Was that it, then? Had he gone to Portugal to track down a prince who had been dead for four hundred years?

All I knew for certain was that I had to find out.

The next morning, Albert drove me and Fr. Jean-Marie to Saint-Malo, stopping first in the nearby village to send a telegram to Paris. While we waited in the barouche, Albert entered the little stone building labeled *Bureau de Poste*. Fr. Jean-Marie and I spent a few minutes in pleasant conversation about the Bretons and their language, and the door opened and out came Albert. As he walked towards us, Fr. Jean-Marie exclaimed, "*Ma foi!*"

"Is something wrong, Father?" I asked.

"It may be nothing at all," replied the priest. To Albert, as he climbed into the barouche, he said,

"Did you see Guillaume Fernais just now, as you left the *Bureau de Poste*?"

"Guillaume Fernais?" repeated Albert. "*Non, Père.*"

"Seeing you exit," Fr. Jean-Marie explained, "he went in very hastily himself." He turned to me. "Guillaume is no Breton. He is from Normandy. He has already been heard saying that France would be better off run by Germans, and he has a . . . *bien ai-mée*, a sweetheart working at the *Bureau de Poste.*"

Albert put a dignified expression upon his face. "Even Fernais would not dare to read a confidential telegram to the Minister of War, and Corinne would not allow him."

"Probably not," mused Fr. Jean-Marie. "Even so, Monsieur McCracken, be very careful in Portugal. Already, the enemy may know of your mission."

CHAPTER 3

AN ADVENTURE IN PORTUGAL

The ship I took was a two-masted packet steamer with a single red and black funnel between the masts, a slightly aging lady of about 535 feet, with a beam of 64. She was propelled by a pair of screws operated by quadruple-expansion steam engines, lovely work that had been completed, I guessed, in the Workman Clark shipyard in Belfast, a guess that was confirmed when I was permitted down into the engine room to marvel at the polished brass and gleaming oil.

The steamer took me around the rocky coast of Brittany, then along the gentler shores of Aquitaine, with its wide, sandy beaches and medieval ports. Spain was a place of yellow rocks, and occasionally snowy mountains glimpsed in the interior. Then the steamer turned south along the Portuguese coast, with its gleaming white houses spilling down the verdant slopes towards the sea.

To be honest, though, I spent most of the five days' voyage with the engineer, whom I found to be a fellow-countryman named McAndrew. He boasted of once having had a long conversation with the novelist and poet Rudyard Kipling, but boasted more of his engines. He was a Presbyterian and something of an amateur theologian, seeing predestination in the stride of the connecting rod, and the Hand of the Almighty in the coupler-flange and spindle-guide.

"Ye'll remember, Mr. McCracken, the story in the Guid Buik aboot Mary and Martha?" he said. "Aboot how Our Laird told Mary, who sat and leestened to Him, that she had the better portion? Well, the Sons of Mary smile and are blessed—they ken the Angels are on their side, ye see. They know Grace is with them, and the Mercies multiplied. They're the ones as sit at the feet of Our Laird—they hear the Guid Word—they see how truly the Promise runs. But they see it because they have cast their burden upon the Laird, and the Laird—well, He lays it on Martha's Sons—on the likes of ye and me, Mr. McCracken!"

I laughed with him about the sins of Mary's Children (I thought of Ari and her books) and the hard-pressed world of Martha's Children, and we sipped Scotch and passed many wonderful hours together.

All too soon, the voyage came to an end, and I found myself disembarking in Lisbon and making for the French consulate, where I picked up some money for my expenses, and learned that French agents were even now searching for Fr. Jamie. He had last been seen in southern Portugal, and having read the *Encyclopaedia Britannica* I knew what that meant—he was heading off to Villa do Infante to investigate Prince Henrique the Navigator.

So I took a train from Lisbon, to the end of the line—Lagos, on the south coast. Most people sleep or read on the train, but I never do. My senses come alive as the train rattles along, shaking me gently this way and that, and I watch the telegraph poles flit past, listen to the rhythmic thumping of the wheels, and smell the oil and the coal.

About halfway through my trip, a young Turk entered my compartment and sat down opposite me. He was a fellow of an exceptionally handsome and even debonair appearance, with a thin, dark moustache along his upper lip and deep-set, dark eyes, who watched me sullenly most of the time. This puzzled me at first, but then I remembered another piece of information I had picked up at the French consulate—that the Turks had now entered the War on the side of the Germans. We were technically enemies, that Turk and I, although we traveled on neutral ground. I ignored him, and watched the telegraph poles. As the journey progressed, an invisible cloud emanated from him, the compartment filling with the aroma of stale Turkish tobacco.

Getting out of the train at the almost impossibly idyllic town of Lagos, I began right away to search for the nearest church. Fr. Jamie, I reasoned, would have to stay somewhere, and most likely he would stay with a brother priest. I had to ask several people before I could get any directions I could understand, and set off through narrow cobbled streets between yellow and white houses. Market stalls were set up along the streets, but the vendors were shutting up for the night. I could smell salt on the air and hear the cry of gulls.

Turning the last corner, I saw, as I expected, the church ahead of me. It was a small white-walled church with terracotta tiles and a bell-tower directly above the door. I quickened my pace towards it.

But before I reached it, I heard a footstep behind me. I tried to turn, but a voice spoke in my ear, while at the same time I was engulfed in the odour of stale Turkish tobacco: "Say nothing, McCracken Bey. Just turn down the side-street on your right."

Nothing quite makes you feel like you're on an adventure like a Luger in the ribs.

It was a dark alley into which the Turk pushed me, deserted except for the rats gnawing at the rubbish overspilling the bins, and deeply shadowed. At the midpoint along the alley stood a knot of six men, all Turks, some wearing fezzes. They turned as we approached, and their movement revealed a seventh figure: a large man in a cassock and priestly collar, heavy-set, with a thick, bushy beard.

"Cracky!" hooted Fr. Jamie. "Och man, it's grand to see you—it's been a long time."

"It's good to see you too, Father," I said. "I was looking for you."

"Were you now? It looks like you've found me."

"I wish we could have met under better circumstances."

"And what's wrong with these circumstances, I'd like to know?" demanded Fr. Jamie, and I felt a sinking feeling, for I knew a theology lesson was coming on. "This is the place the Almighty has chosen for me to be, and I'm happy here. As a journalist friend of mine said, not long ago, an inconvenience is just an adventure wrongly considered."

"What do you think we should do?" I wondered.

"Oh, that doesna matter, lad," replied the priest. "We'll think of something. We've been in worse scrapes after closing time in Aberdeen. But we ought to ask these kind gentlemen what they want." He turned to one of his captors, a man with a white scar from one cheek to the other across his nose. "Well, Nazif, what is it you want from me?"

Nazif had a large knife in his hand, and it glinted in the dim light. Leaning close to Fr. Jamie, he snarled, "You know what we want, Erickson Bey."

Fr. Jamie looked back at me. "I think he wants to convert," he smiled. With a snarl, Nazif struck Fr. Jamie across the cheek with the back of his hand. I started forward, but was restrained by the handsome Turk's Luger thrusting under my ribs. Fr. Jamie rubbed his cheek briefly where the blow had landed. "I think he'll make a pretty poor catechumen, though. Do you know what they want from us, Cracky?"

"Do I have to answer that, Father?" I replied carefully.

"Well, of course you have to answer!" retorted Fr. Jamie impatiently. "When a priest asks you a direct question, lad, you answer it."

"I might want to equivocate," I answered. "Remember the stories you told us kids of those Jesuit priests in Queen Elizabeth's time?"

"Those priests were in mortal danger, lad." I made a helpless gesture towards the knives and Lugers. "Och, that's nothing at all. Still, if you feel—"

"Erickson Bey!" snarled Nazif, raising his knife close to Fr. Jamie's face. "Be silent!"

"My friend and I are having a little conversation about theology," replied Fr. Jamie mildly. "It's a very subtle problem—"

"Be silent!" shouted the Turk. "Answer question!"

Fr. Jamie gave a little sigh. I had seen that expression before, when little Robbie McTavish had asked how much sin he was permitted to commit and still be able to go to Heaven. Fr. Jamie said, "Now, how can I answer your question if I have to be silent? Do you understand semaphore? Or sign language?"

"Silence!" shrieked Nazif, stepping so close to Fr. Jamie that his nose almost touched the big priest's chin.

In a flash, Fr. Jamie caught Nazif by the wrist and twisted. Nazif cried out in pain, and the knife spun from his grip. With his other hand, Fr. Jamie delivered a right cross to the Turk's nose that dropped him instantly, unconscious.

I took my cue from Fr. Jamie and, reaching behind me, grabbed my escort by the arm and spun him at his companions. He hit them like a bowling ball, and they scattered like skittles. One of the Lugers went off with a blinding flash and a roar that filled the alley and made my ears ring. The bullet slammed into the wall behind me. I leaped at the Turk who had fired and pummeled him to the ground. Another Turk jumped me from behind, but with a duck of my head and shoulders I threw him off. Another gunshot crashed out in the narrow alleyway, but I heard a more satisfying crack as Fr. Jamie landed yet another punch.

My opponent being down and unconscious, I sprang to my feet, swinging my fist at the nearest of the Turks. My knuckles connected with his jaw, and he staggered backwards. I followed with a left, and he collapsed like a stick bridge in a hurricane. I looked around for another, and saw Fr. Jamie swinging his fist at the debonair fellow who had conducted me to this place. He spun away, his hands flying up to his face. The others lay groaning on the ground, or else completely unconscious.

"Come on, Cracky," urged Fr. Jamie, pulling me away from the carnage. "Let's be going."

We dashed off down the alleyway, turned, and turned again. He never paused to think and never doubled back—he seemed to know the seamy backstreets of Lagos well. After some time, we found ourselves in a more highly populated place, a wide street where the lamp-lighter was just beginning to reach up with his long pole and a few after-dinner walkers were out for a stroll. At last, Fr. Jamie slowed to a stop, threw his head back, and guffawed heartily.

"Ah, Cracky, I'm glad you turned up when you did!" he said, wiping his eyes. "I don't think I could have handled those last two."

We laughed together for a while, until my eyes streamed with tears and my sides ached. At length, we proceeded at a calmer pace, and Fr. Jamie said, "Sorry, lad, that I pressed you to answer just now. I should have guessed you knew what they wanted, and didn't want to let on."

"The truth is," I said, "I do know what they want, and that's the reason I'm here trying to find you."

Fr. Jamie snatched a glance up and down the street. "Dinna say a word here, lad," he urged. "We'll have to find a place a little more private than this."

"Where are you staying?" I asked.

"With a friend of mine," Fr. Jamie replied, "a Jesuit. But I canna go back there now, can I? Och, you're naught but a wee bairn in this adventuring business yet, lad." He thought for a moment, then said, "I know a place we can get a drink and talk. It's a bit rough, but not with the kind of folk we want to avoid, and if there's any trouble, I know I can depend on these lads to help out."

"How do you get to know these places, Father?" I asked.

"Well, in between my researches, I try to save a few souls, you ken," he replied, and led me off the main street once again.

It was quite a walk, and the sky was dark by the time we reached the docks. I could hear the lapping of the waves against the wharf, and the masts stood out sharp against the starry sky. I followed Fr. Jamie along the dock until he stopped outside a narrow door over which the words *Cantina Marinheiros* were painted in flaking paint.

"Oh, I am an ancient minister, and I stoppeth one in three," Fr. Jamie announced, pushing open the door. "'By your bushy beard and glittering eye, now wherefore stopp'st thou me?' 'The Bridegroom's doors are opened wide, and I am next of kin; the guests are met, the feast is set; will ye no come in wi' me?'"

We found ourselves in a narrow, smoky room. The bar was a series of barrels, each with a tap, in front of which stood a heavy-set man with a bald head and a thick, greying moustache. The room was full of tables, about half of which were occupied by an unruly collection of sailors. One of them, stumping back from the bar with frothing ales in his hands, actually sported a peg leg. At one end of the room, a pretty girl sang to the accompaniment of an accordion.

Fr. Jamie threaded his way through the tables, greeting left and right as he went, with a comment in Portuguese for each one we greeted. We reached the bar, and the bartender came beaming over to us. "*Padre!*" he cried out, and then embarked on a stream of Portuguese out of which I couldn't make a single word. The dialogue culminated with the bartender pouring out a couple of glasses of rum. Fr. Jamie pushed one of them along the bar to me, explaining apologetically, "It's a wee bit rough, but you get used to it. Nothing like the old Axe and Cat back in Aberdeen." He slammed his drink and handed the glass back to the bartender. When it had been re-filled, he led me to one of the tables near a dark window.

"Now, lad," said Fr. Jamie, keeping a sharp eye on the door, "I think you'd better tell me what's going on."

In as few words as possible, I told him about my stay with Jaubert in Brittany, about Millerand's visit, about the strange fabric out of which the manuscript page was made, and the strange symbols. I told him about Ari, and her perplexity. And then I told him about Zun.

Fr. Jamie didn't say anything for a long while. He looked like Sir Galahad, seeing at long last the Holy Grail. He gulped down half his rum and then said, "Well, Cracky, you've discovered a thing I've been looking for all my life. An actual artifact from the Land of Zun. Do you have it with you?"

"I don't," I replied.

"You left it with your lady wife, then, I'd wager?"

"I did."

"Well, that was wise, but it puts her in some danger. The sooner we can join up with her, the better. Oh, Cracky!" he rhapsodized, "you've made this old man of God a happy cleric this night, so you have!"

"But what *is* Zun?" I asked.

His bushy eyebrows met over his nose in a sudden frown. "Were you not paying attention when I told you back in Aberdeen?"

"No," I said, then hurriedly corrected myself: "Yes I was, but it was a long time ago, and I've forgotten."

Fr. Jamie drew a deep breath. "We'll need another round of drinks," he said, "for 'tis a long tale in the telling." He looked at me more closely. "Come on, lad, I've bought the first round. Don't be a skinflint, now."

When I'd bought the drinks, Fr. Jamie sighed long, and stared into space a few moments. Then he said, "We'd best start with Dom Henrique—Henry the Navigator, that is."

"I've read about him," I said, and summarized for him what I'd gleaned from the encyclopaedia. "He was trying to find the Land of Prester John," I concluded.

"That's a grand beginning," said Fr. Jamie. "And you should know from the start that Zun is the local name for the Land of Prester John—I say local, but of course nobody knows where it is. It's been a lost valley for centuries."

"And who was Prester John?" I inquired. "I remember the emerald sceptre and the army of cannibals."

"Now, if you'd followed up that reference in a different volume of the *Encyclopaedia Britannica*," said Fr. Jamie, "you'd not have to ask me such blithering questions. Prester John was a Christian king, who ruled a land of fabulous wealth, surrounded by Moslem kingdoms. At the time when St. Bernard of Clairvaux was preaching the Second Crusade, Prester John saw an opportunity to assist his western Christian brothers. Amassing a vast army, he emerged from his lost valley, defeated the kings of

Medes and Persia, and marched towards the Holy Land, intent on liberating Jerusalem from the Turks.

"He never reached Jerusalem. When he reached the River Tigris, he was unable to cross, for he had brought no boats with him. Hearing that further north the river was iced over, he marched in that direction. His army, he reasoned, could cross the Tigris on the ice. But he found no place where the ice was strong enough to support the weight of his army, so they sat down on the banks of the Tigris and waited. But winter closed in and, although the river still flowed freely south, his men began to die of cold and hunger. In the end, reluctantly, Prester John turned around and went home to Zun. He was never heard of again.

"More than fifty years later, the Pope sent missionaries to the Mongols, and these missionaries asked after Prester John. But the Mongols had heard nothing, they said, of the Land of Zun or Prester John. Puzzled, the Pope looked elsewhere for a possible location for the Land of Zun, and rumours reached him that a Christian king ruled amidst heathen kingdoms in Abyssinia."

"So I suppose Henrique never located the Land of Zun?" I said.

"Right—he died in 1460, thirty years before Columbus discovered the New World, and he had not found the Land of Prester John, the Lost Valley of Zun."

"Is that the end of the story?" I asked.

"Is that the end of the story?" Fr. Jamie echoed. "No, it isn't the end of the story. That would be a depressing end to a story. 'Did he live happily ever after, Father?' 'No, he died a disillusioned old man.' Fortunately, there were others who continued Dom Henrique's work."

"Well, who were they?"

"If you'll quit your fashing, I'll tell you." Fr. Jamie eyed his empty glass meaningfully. "I'm a wee bit dry, too," he said. "It's a great wonder, how rum will wet your whistle."

And so I had to go and get a couple more drinks before he would resume his tale.

CHAPTER 4
THE TEAM GATHERS

B ut Fr. Jamie could not continue the story at once. We were interrupted by a sailor, who had just arrived from Shanghai, and who prevailed upon him to hear his confession at once. Fr. Jamie took out his stole, and left me alone, sipping at my rum, for over half an hour. I couldn't help reflecting on how the sailor's sins must have accumulated in Shanghai, a port city famed for sins, according to my recollection. The cantina was quiet by the time the sailor was finished and Fr. Jamie returned. The bartender brought over a couple of glasses of rum, which the sailor from Shanghai had bought.

"His penance?" I asked, taking a sip from the new glass.

"Cracky!" said Fr. Jamie, shocked. "You tease me unmercifully, as always. Of course it's not his penance. That would not be proper at all, now, would it? But I can't stem the gratitude of my impromptu flock. Now, where was I?"

"Dom Henrique had just died, without finding Zun."

"Oh, aye, I remember now. Well, the new king of Portugal, João II, was also interested in finding

Zun. He wanted to find a safe trade route through the Moslem lands to India, where his merchants could buy gems, and spices, and gold. Working at first with the Church, he sent missionaries east into Asia and south into Abyssinia, but either they never came back or else they came back empty-handed. The king thought to himself, If the men of God cannot do this work, perhaps what we're looking for is an adventurer, someone who knows languages, someone who's prepared to take a risk.

"Now, there was a man working for King João called Pero da Covilha. Pero was a squire at the king's court, but João noticed that he had a talent for languages, and so he sent him on a number of diplomatic missions. He was ambassador to Morocco, he negotiated a treaty with the king of Tlemecen, he purchased horses for Duke Manuel of Beja. He even spied on the king of Castile for João. In all this, Pero was faithful and successful and, more to the point, João noticed that he was lucky. So he commissioned Pero to accompany another adventurer, Afonso de Paiva, to discover the Land of Prester John."

"Let me guess," I ventured. "He was never heard of again?"

"Och, you will be spoiling the story, will you not, Cracky?" chided Fr. Jamie. "As it happens, there's a lot more to tell."

"Then tell it."

"No. I'm a bit offended."

"All right, you old barm-pot!" I said. "I'm sorry I interrupted your story. Will you please, please, *please* proceed with it?"

"I'll think about it," replied Fr. Jamie; and after about half a second, he added: "All right, you great wally. I'll tell you the rest.

"Pero and Afonso left Portugal in 1487, bound for Cairo, where they were to split up—Afonso was to go south to the Christian realm in Abyssinia, while Pero would travel east to seek Prester John beyond the River Tigris."

"And *then* they were never seen again," I said with definitiveness.

"Och, you wee maddy walloper, you have a fine ear for a cliché," said Fr. Jamie. "Were it not for your generosity with the rum, now, I'd be saying goodbye to you and going on my way. But I've a mind to return a fair deed for a fair deed, so whisht now and let me finish.

"Some years passed, and King João began to wonder what had become of his intrepid adventurers. He employed two Jews, a rabbi named Abraham and Joseph, a shoemaker, to sail to Cairo in search of them. Off they went, and a couple of years later they returned. They had seen Afonso, they said. In fact, they had been with him when he had died. Afonso told them that he and Pero had agreed to travel in search of the Land of Prester John for three years, and then meet in Cairo once more. Afonso had

40

reached Cairo at the time appointed, but Pero had not come back.

"Now, here's the curious thing, lad," said Fr. Jamie, leaning close across the table, "and the thing I've only just found out. Pero da Covilha had left his wife and unborn son behind to go adventuring for the king. When Rabbi Abraham and Joseph returned with their tale, the king assumed that Pero was dead too, and he sent a messenger with his condolences, and a generous sum of money in reparation, to the widow. But she wasna there. She and the bairn just—vanished."

"So neither Pero nor his wife were ever seen again?"

"Aye, that's the long and the short of it, lad. I'd always known Pero was a married man, but it wasn't until this trip to Portugal that I discovered his wife had disappeared. I'd always thought Pero had died in Asia, but I'd bet everything I own (which is almost nothing) that she went out to Zun to join him there."

"So that's what the Turks wanted from you?" I asked.

Fr. Jamie shrugged. "I haven't a clue what that pack of wallies was after. I thought you might be able to explain that, Cracky."

I cast my mind back over the last few days. I remembered Guillaume Fernais, back in Brittany. I said, "I cabled the French Minister to update him on what I was doing. It's possible that the telegram was intercepted by the Germans. They may have set the Turks on us, learning that I was looking for you. They may have believed you knew more than you do."

"Well, I've only a tad more information now than before. Knowing that Pero's wife disappeared doesna tell me where she is. Perhaps this manuscript of your lady wife's will tell us more. Where is she now?"

"We planned to meet in Marseilles, and she's trying to get hold of our friend, a Russian who's been rebuilding the airship we acquired last year."

"Marseilles, is it? D'you mind if I tag along?"

"I was hoping you would," I replied. "When do you have to be back in Aberdeen?"

"I've another month or so of leave owing to me," he answered. "I'll need to be back at the New Year."

And so we had a plan: a trip to Marseilles, where we could look at the fabric and unravel the web of mystery surrounding the Land of Zun.

The War had not yet made travel through Portugal and Spain impossible, and we were able to catch a train to Lisbon, where we had to stay overnight before catching the express to Marseilles. I say *express*, but the Spanish train was a real bone-rattler with wooden seats that jarred against our spines every time we passed over the points or even the joins in the tracks. It was a charming engine, though: I felt I was in touch with its heartbeat as we chugged along through the desert or beside the sea.

We changed trains at the border with France because Spain uses a narrower gauge of track than the other European countries. That necessitated another night's stay, and we began our journey through southern France early the next morning, pulling into the magnificent station late in the afternoon.

The train came to a hissing halt, and we all lurched forward. There was the customary pause, like that delicious moment of anticipation between turning the crank and the motor-car's engine roaring into life, then all the passengers in the compartment got, stretching, out of their seats, reaching for their luggage.

Fr. Jamie and I made our way along the passageway, our suitcases bumping against the walls, then stepped down onto the platform. Amidst the clouds of smoke and steam, I caught sight of Ari. Our eyes clicked, and she made a determined path towards us.

"Charmed, my dear," said Fr. Jamie, when I had made the introductions, and he bent to kiss her hand. "When Cracky here described you to me, which he did at length during our train journey, I thought he was surely exaggerating; now I see he was minimizing your beauty so as to surprise and delight me upon our meeting."

"Well, thank you, Father," replied Ari. "Mac, you didn't tell me that some of your friends weren't thugs."

"Truth be known," I said, "Fr. Jamie's putting it on a bit for you. He's been known to behave like a thug on occasion too."

"Father," said Ari, as we emerged into the bright sunlight of southern France, "satisfy the curiosity of an ignorant American. You sound Scots to me, but your name is—what? German?"

"Danish, dear lady," replied Fr. Jamie. "I'm from the Shetlands, and there's Viking blood in my veins, as you can tell from my partiality for a tot of mead now and then."

"I can testify to that," I commented, "and to his partiality for Scotch or rum at all other times."

We descended the magnificent staircase outside the station. It had obelisks on either side and street lamps running down its middle. At the foot of the stairs was the road, and there was the Daimler, Fritz at attention beside it. "Welcome back, Herr McCracken," said Fritz, beaming.

A few moments later, we were motoring through the teeming streets of Marseilles. A few more turns, and we found ourselves bumping over a dirt track to an open field. The leaves were beginning to turn, imparting a beautiful gold to the trees that edged the field.

And in the middle of the field was the LS3, the airship Sikorsky and we owned. He had spent almost a year building a new envelope around the gondola, which had barely survived our last adventure. I could see Sikorsky, at work beneath the gondola. He had a team of mechanics hauling great oil drums up the ramp into the coach house, which was normally reserved for the Daimler.

Fritz pressed the brakes, and the Daimler rolled to a halt. Sikorsky strode forward, smiling from ear to ear.

"McCracken!" he shouted. "Is very good to see you!" And he folded me in that Russian bear hug of his and kissed me on each cheek.

"What's going on here?" I asked, pointing at the mechanics with the oil drums.

"Extra fuel—carriage house is only place to store it. This time, we go far, we need more fuel—Daimler cannot come with us."

"Too bad," I said, "but perhaps we won't need it." I looked up at the envelope. "It looks like good work to me," I said.

"Ah, here you see nothing," answered the Russian. "Wait till you see inside."

"I don't want to dampen the scientific enthusiasm of you boys," said Ari, joining the conversation with Fr. Jamie at her side, "but there's something else we need to do first." She reached into her handbag and drew out something bluish-white, overwritten with black, and folded into a square.

"Is that the Zunian manuscript?" asked Fr. Jamie, his eyes lighting up.

"It is," said Ari. "Let's get up into the gondola."

Fritz was driving the Daimler away and the sun was setting as we climbed the steps into the LS3's gondola, Ari leading us with the mysterious manuscript in her hand.

S hortly after we entered the *Speiseraum*, or dining room of the LS3, Fritz appeared. His face
was still dark with dirt, except the two white
circles around his eyes, where his goggles had
been. These circles drew attention to his strange
eyes, that seemed to look in different directions. He
poured whiskies for Fr. Jamie and me, champagne
for Ari, and vodka for Sikorsky. We toasted our new
enterprise, and then sat down at a table in the middle
of the panoramic windows at the stern of the gondola. We could see the pleasant scenery of southern
France all around us, and the skyline of Marseilles
on the horizon.

The *Speiseraum* was semi-circular in shape, with
windows all about the curved wall and a fully
stocked bar along the flat wall. It was the sternmost
of the compartments on the lower deck of the LS3.
To the fore of it was the carriage house where we
normally stored the Daimler, but now fuel. Forward
of that were the galley, radio and navigation rooms,
and the wheel-house, the latter completely surrounded by glass. The cabins and a workshop were
on the upper deck, which was housed inside the
four-hundred-foot-long cigar-shaped envelope.

This envelope also housed three huge ballonets containing the hydrogen that gave the airship its buoyancy. The LS3 had been designed by a German of genius but of dubious morals, Fritz's former boss, and it had fallen to Jaubert, Sikorsky, and us by default when its owner had died whilst pretending to be somewhere else—don't ask me any more details, it's a long story.

Ari spread the manuscript out on the table. Fr. Jamie sighed and, leaning forward, traced a few of the characters with a tender forefinger. After a few moments, he looked up.

"This is no language I'm familiar with, I'm afraid," he said.

"I haven't been able to find anything quite like it," answered Ari. "It seems to be very old, and bears some resemblance to modern Kyrgyz."

"Ah!" cried Sikorsky. "Is language of Kazakhs!"

"Yes, but this must be several centuries old," said Ari. "I looked up a few things about how Turkish has changed since the Middle Ages, and applied similar changes backwards to Kyrgyz, and I came up with a way of more or less interpreting this." She reached again into her handbag and drew out a folded piece of foolscap paper. "It's very shaky as a translation—I wouldn't want to publish it—but it probably gives a rough idea." She placed the paper on top of the manuscript, and we all looked at the penciled series of half-lines.

> Presbyter Cuan, by the grace of God
> Pero Duke of Guzelvadi, his most
> because we know that you
> Portugal we think it fitting
> Zun who knows not the secret path
> of Khoramdin, near the place whence
> Eve were expelled from Paradise
> direction he must walk along the
> city of Babel, where once a tower
> east from Babel he will find Monday City
> find Sea of Rocks, which is fed by
> there be no water. Follow the Stony
> sunrise in the west there he will stop
> in brief therefore God willing
> gratitude which you deserve for
> us and with the full intention of
> return to Zun we ask you to continue
> Given at the holy city of Bashkent
> in the year of Our Lord mcccclxxxxvi

"Well, that's clear enough," I remarked. "Why don't we get started at once?"

Ari stuck out her tongue at me, and Fr. Jamie said, "Will you whisht now, you great gormless wally, and let me think!" He pointed to the top. "Presbyter Cuan—that's Prester John. Cuan is the way it was pronounced back then, like *Juan* in modern Spanish. *By the grace of God* sounds like the opening salutation of a letter. It would go something like, 'Prester John, by the grace of God king of Zun, to

49

Pero, Duke of Guzelvadi, his most faithful servant.' And look at that Roman numeral at the end: 1496." He peered closely at the manuscript then, looking up at the rest of us, his face broke into a wide grin. "Och, to think that the wee laddie himself, Pero da Covilha, carried this letter with him. Duke of Guzelvadi—he was a duke in Zun. As I thought—he visited Portugal to bring his wife and bairn to Zun." He picked up the manuscript and held it up to the light to examine it with an almost beatific countenance. "It looks as if Prester John gave him this as directions back to Zun. That's interesting." He pointed to the fifth line of Ari's text. "'Zun who knows not the secret path.' I'd reckon that originally read something like, 'No one can come to Zun who knows not the secret path.'"

"Eve expelled from Paradise and Babel, where once was a tower," I said. "Does anyone really know where Eden and Babel were?"

"The best explanations about them suggest they were in Mesopotamia," said Ari, "between the rivers Euphrates and Tigris."

"Is strange," said Sikorsky, frowning. "This Khoramdin I have heard of."

"It's a different language from most of the text," explained Ari, "so I thought it would be a personal name. In fact, it's Persian, and means *of the joyful religion.*"

Sikorsky snapped his fingers. "There are freedom fighters called Khoramdin, a thousand years ago, perhaps more. They live in Azerbaijan, in south of Russia, between Black Sea and Caspian Sea."

Ari's eyes lit up. "This may be a long shot," she said, "but I was reading not long ago how nearly all the languages in Europe developed out of one language, spoken ten thousand years ago, a kind of grandfather of most of the modern languages of Europe and Asia. As the speakers of that language migrated in all different directions, their languages began to differ from one another until they spoke all sorts of different languages—Latin, Greek, German, the Celtic languages, even Sanskrit. But all those languages are related to one another. The ancient language, the grandfather language, originated somewhere in the vicinity of the Caspian Sea." We all looked at her uncomprehendingly. "Don't you see?" she said. "That's Babel—where men originally spoke a single language, but God punished their pride by making them unable to speak to one another. The Old Testament story is a mythical rendition of the historical fact that all languages divided somewhere between the Black Sea and the Caspian Sea, ten thousand years ago. Antiquarians have been looking for the Tower of Babel for centuries, but they've been looking in the wrong place. It isn't in Mesopotamia, it's in Azerbaijan.

I sat back in my chair and looked out of the windows at the peaceful French landscape. "Azerbaijan's a long way off," I said. "We'd better get started soon."

We set a course for Baku, the capital of Azerbaijan, because Sikorsky knew someone there, an old friend from his university days, who had gone into the oil business. But we couldn't fly there directly, because the War got in the way. We flew south, with the coast of Italy just in view to the port, then across the Mediterranean to Cairo, where we refueled at a French aerodrome.

Cairo was growing smaller in the dining room windows, and I was breakfasting just after Mass with some French toast Fritz had cooked up for me, when Fr. Jamie entered and waved a boisterous good morning to me. We ate, drank coffee, and watched Cairo diminish. The desert was yellow to the left, the sea a dazzling blue to the right. It was beautiful—like bright steel and dark oil.

"So," said Fr. Jamie with that annoying suddenness of his, "you married this very admirable and beautiful lady of yours. Did you tell her your first name?"

"Of course I did," I replied, shifting uneasily in my seat. "I had to—it was on the marriage certificate."

"You drove the poor lass nearly crazy before your wedding, you ken."

"It wasn't a long drive," I said, "more a Sunday afternoon excursion."

Fr. Jamie poked me hard on the shoulder. "That's no way to speak of your wife, the woman God Himself selected as your life's companion, you ungrateful wally!" A little more mildly, he went on, "I hear she took a trip to Aberdeen a little before you got hitched, to take a wee peek at the parish register at St. Joseph's. And do you ken what the poor girl found there?"

I sniggered. "Yes, I do."

"Och, lad, you should be ashamed of yourself," he reproached me. "To cut out a piece of the parish register is an act of vandalism against church property, and you'll roast for years in Purgatory, so you will, on account of it. Are you not ashamed of yourself, man?"

I hadn't been until then, but Fr. Jamie's wrath was somewhat sobering. I mumbled an apology.

"Well," said Fr. Jamie, rising with a frown, "I'm glad the poor lassie knows what to call her man now, but I think you've shown a shameful streak in your so-called character." He bored into me with his dark eyes. "So I have spoken," he said, making the sign of the cross, "*in nomine Patris, et Filii, et Spiritu Sancti. Amen.*" And he wheeled about and left the dining room.

Fr. Jamie had killed my appetite, so I put my fork down and left the dining room. I went to find

Ari, feeling for some reason that in some way I had betrayed her.

Another day's flying brought us to Baku, a city whose supplies of petroleum seemed inexhaustible. I stood beside Sikorsky as we flew over the city. Everywhere we looked, we could see the strange pyramids that housed the oil drills, fields upon fields of them. Orange flames burned at the top of many of them, trailing off into thick, oily smoke, grasping with ragged black fingers at the sun. The derricks, oil refineries and warehouses of modern design clutched at parts of the old city—narrow streets, wide marketplaces, spindly minarets—leaving their smudgy fingerprints everywhere. Out on the Caspian Sea squatted a fleet of oil tankers. Strands of darkness, which seemed to be minor oil spills, reached out from the fleet through the paler waters.

Ari entered the wheel-house, watched me for a moment, and then joined me staring out of the forward windows.

"This is not what it's supposed to be like," I told her. "This isn't engineering—it's just greed." I struggled for the words. "It's as if Martha's Sons went mad, and forgot *why* they were working." Ari's eyebrows pursed in inquiry. I explained what the ship's engineer had told me on the voyage to Portugal.

Ari linked her arm in mine and rested her head on my shoulder. "I know, dear," she said. "It's a fallen world."

We touched down at the aerodrome in the late afternoon. We could see a little blue sky overhead, but a black cloud lay over the city itself, as if gathering it jealously away from the healthier air. Sikorsky instantly set about procuring more fuel, so as to leave our reserves untapped for the moment. He didn't have to worry about getting enough. There was plenty of it about: we could smell petroleum in the air we breathed, taste it in our mouths, feel it cloying in our hair.

I ambled over to Sikorsky. A crew was refueling us, while he had been talking to a man in a white suit, streaked and smeared with oil. "McCracken," he said as I approached, "this man, Sergei Andreivich, he have a motor-car. We borrow, and go to see my friend, Vladimir Petrovich Zhukovsky." He turned to the man. "You know where we can find Bari Engineering Company, *da*?" There followed a quick exchange in Russian or Ukrainian, I couldn't tell which, then the man strode off and came back, soon after, in a motor-car. It must have been built locally, because I didn't recognize the type. Its cabin was enclosed, and the paint was dull and dirty, the tyres nearly bald, and the lamps dark and unburnished. It would have been a sweet little motor-car, but no one seemed to have been proud enough of it to take proper care. I patted the poor thing on the fender and whispered a few encouraging words to it, while Sikorsky jumped into the driver's seat. I slipped in next to him, and Ari and Fr. Jamie climbed into the back.

The Bari Engineering Company stood on a promontory, a mass of steel spires and drums, interspersed with wooden shacks. At the gate, Sikorsky inquired after his friend, shouting to be heard over the clamour of the machinery. The man on the gate pointed, and we clattered over the rough ground towards one of the wooden buildings.

"Vladimir Petrovich study chemical engineering at Kiev Polytechnic," Sikorsky explained to me. "I study mechanical engineering. His father want him to make much money."

He parked the motor-car outside the wooden building, and we all climbed out. The windows were grimy with oil, and words in Cyrillic letters, which I assumed meant BARI ENGINEERING COMPANY, were barely discernible through the muck. Sikorsky pushed on the door and we all followed him into the building.

Inside, it seemed like an army of typists had gathered for a parade: there were rows of them, all clacking away, while smartly-dressed men wove their way between them, like shuttles threading through a loom. One of the nearest of these men looked up as we entered. For a moment, he regarded us with incomprehension, then his features exploded in a wide smile.

"Vasili Ivanovich!" he cried, and ran forward to wrap Sikorsky in a warm embrace, kissing him on either cheek. They talked for a few moments in Russian, then Sikorsky turned to me.

"Vladimir Petrovich," he said, "these are my very good friends, McCracken, Ariadne, Fr. Jamie Erickson." Zhukovsky nodded and shook hands with each of us in turn.

"Let us go to my office," he said. "There, is much quieter."

He led us off through the typists to an office at the back of the wide room. Closing the door, he cut off much of the clamour, and smiled at us. He was a handsome man in his late thirties, with a thick wave of dark hair, neatly combed, and a diamond-shaped beard that had the effect of making his wide forehead seem vast. He wore a brown suit with a high collar and a tie with a silver pin.

"This is great pleasure to me," he said. "It is very long time since last we meet, *nyet*?"

"You have done well, Vladik," remarked Sikorsky, looking about the office. There was a thick carpet on the floor, a leather-topped desk with an array of blotters, envelopes, gold pens, and sheaves of paper.

Zhukovsky gave a sigh and lowered himself into the chair behind the desk. "Oil business bring much money," he said, "but little happiness. All is money, money, money, and dirt, dirt, dirt. Many days pass, and I see nothing of the sun. I make much money, but can it repay me for living in such ugliness? And I am the cause of this ugliness. Is this what we were made for, Vasya? Is this why we studied all those years? Why must I suffer so?"

Sikorsky reached forward and slapped his friend on the shoulder. "Vladik," he said, "stop talking like character in Dostoevsky novel! Is no good. Be cheerful! Now—stop to whine and help us with our problem."

"What is it you need, Vasili Ivanovich?" Zhukovsky asked, somewhat calmed by his friend's onslaught.

Ari took out her transcript of the Kyrgyz manuscript and read aloud the lines that were relevant to our stay in Azerbaijan. Zhukovsky nodded wisely when he had listened.

"Is true, Vasili Ivanovich," he said, "these words speak of Azerbaijan. In spare time, which is very little, I study something of Azerbaijan, its people, its customs, its history. Khoramdin was local rebel, or freedom fighter. They are Persian warriors, and they live many centuries ago in the hills west of here. They fight against Ottomans when they try to take the country for themselves."

"Was there some kind of a stronghold they might have fought from?" asked Fr. Jamie.

Zhukovsky replied, "Father, the Khoramdin fight from many strongholds, hidden throughout mountains. Some of them, no human eye has seen for hundreds of years."

"The other clue we have," said Ari, "is that Eve was driven from Paradise near it."

Zhukovsky's eyebrows rose. "Ah," he said, "that explain much. There is ancient legend that Garden of Eden was in Persia, in the city of Tabriz. Fifty mile from Tabriz is Babak Fort, stronghold of one of the chiefs of Khoramdin. This place is in mountains, built on top of very high peak—is very difficult to get to."

"Babak Fort," I said. "Can you give us a precise location?"

Zhukovsky opened a drawer, rifled it a few moments, and produced a map, which he spread out on the table-top, pushing aside his blotter to create more space. "See," he said, pointing. "Babak Fort is here, almost two hundred miles southwest. But is across very difficult terrain. You will need camels, my friends, horses, food, water."

"Or an airship," I said.

"Ah—the airship, she is yours? I see her arrive today. It gives me joy in the heart to see her. Yes, in airship, journey is very easy." He folded up the map and returned it to the desk drawer. "But now, my friends," he said, "you will join me, and my family, for dinner this evening?"

We all agreed with enthusiasm, but Ari insisted that we return to the LS3 to dress properly, and so when Zhukovsky had given Sikorsky directions to his house, we all exited into the motor-car.

"Babak Fort," said Fr. Jamie, once we were bouncing through the narrow streets of Baku.

"Then what?" asked Sikorsky. "Next clue is Tower of Babel. How we find that?"

"There's most likely a clue at Babak Fort," I pointed out.

"But finding the clue will be tough," Ari observed. "Probably, we'll need the part of the manuscript the Turks have."

"So," summarized Fr. Jamie, "they have the clue, but we have the location of the clue. A pretty wee problem."

Night had fallen, but the land was still lit by the fires that burned atop the oil derricks, so when we got back to the aerodrome the huge envelope of the LS3 was visible, picked out in a faint orange sheen. But two hundred yards away, Sikorsky cried out in alarm and switched off the engine.

"What is it, Vasili Ivanovich?" asked Ari. Sikorsky said nothing, but pointed.

A light was on in the LS3. It was not Fritz's cabin, but it was one of the cabins. And it was not a steady light, but the wavering and dim light of an electric torch.

"Mac," said Ari, "somebody's searching our room!"

CHAPTER 6

A PAIR OF TRAPS

We slid out of the motor-car and crept along, low to the ground, hugging the darkness as we approached the LS3. Some oil drums stood in lines, like teeth on a rack-frame, about thirty yards from the gondola, and we paused there, peeping around them. A pair of Turks stood on guard, one on either side of the steps. Each was armed with a Luger, and they scanned the aerodrome, their heads moving back and forth and their eyes glinting as they caught the oil-flames from the derricks.

Behind the oil drums, we consulted with each other quickly. Fr. Jamie was the only one of us who had brought his revolver, so he remained behind the oil drums, where he could see if the Turks inside attempted to escape. The rest of us would circle round behind the guards.

We said a quick prayer together, then Sikorsky went off to the left, Ari and I to the right. We crawled across the hard earth of the aerodrome, our bellies scraping the dirt. The light appeared excessive to me—the whole airfield seemed bathed in the orange glow from the oil fires. It seemed impossible that the Turkish guards would miss us.

I wondered what had happened to Fritz—it seemed likely that he had been captured by the Turks, or worse.

The LS3 began to loom large over our heads. We had almost drawn level with the guards. We crept on, turning inwards slightly so that we approached the Turks at an oblique angle. Now we were behind them—I saw Sikorsky crawling along, twenty yards away. Now we could see their heels, their backs. They were partially screened from us by the mobile steps we had run against the gondola door.

Simultaneously, Ari and I and Sikorsky got to our feet. We each marked our man. Sikorsky nodded once, and we made a dash for it.

I hit the ground just behind my Turk and rolled towards him like a bowling ball. I struck the backs of his legs. He cried out and fell heavily. I rose and punched him in the middle of his face. Ari had already seized his Luger. Meanwhile, Sikorsky had the other around the neck and had dragged him to the ground. He made an attempt to cry out, but Sikorsky clapped his hand over his mouth. With his other hand, Sikorsky beat the Turk's hand against the ground until he dropped the Luger. Then the Russian took it up and struck the Turk across the head with it. He and I dragged both limp Turks behind the steps.

"We should tie them up," I observed.

"No time." Sikorsky waved to Fr. Jamie, who hurried across the dirt towards us. "Ari can guard them."

Ari nodded, leveling her Luger at the inert forms. Leaving her with the unconscious guards, we stole as silently as we could up the steps and into the gondola. Fr. Jamie stood guard and motioned for Sikorsky and me to go fore and aft. I checked the carriage house and found nothing but barrels of fuel, then moved back to the dining room.

It was a mess. They had pulled everything apart. In fact, the place stank of spilled whisky and rum, as they had smashed all the bottles, the glasses, everything. Chairs and tables were upended, the pictures had been pulled from the wall behind the bar and thrown onto the ground, and all the cupboard doors had been wrenched open, the contents spilled over the floor.

They'll wish they hadn't done that, I thought grimly.

Back in the passageway, Fr. Jamie gestured for us to follow him, and he crept slowly up the steps to the top deck. At the top, Sikorsky turned left to search the workshop, Fr. Jamie and I right to the cabins.

Half the doors were open. From the last one on the right we could hear a noise of things being thrown on the floor, and we could see the light waving to and fro. Fr. Jamie and I advanced down the hallway. We took a quick glance into each cabin as we passed it. Each was a mess, the contents of the drawers and cupboards strewn over the floors. This would take hours to clean up, I thought, dismayed.

We reached the last cabins. Ari's and mine was on the starboard, Fritz's on the port. Each of them was being searched. I could smell cheap Turkish tobacco, and knew that the debonair Turk from the train and from the streets of Lagos was in there.

Sikorsky re-joined us. He had visited the armoury, and handed me a revolver. I thumbed back the safety.

The click seemed to echo through the empty hallway.

"Now!" shouted Fr. Jamie. The three of us sprang into the cabins. Sikorsky was beside me as we barged into my own and Ari's cabin.

We had chosen correctly. Two men were in the cabin: Nazif and the debonair Turk. The latter was just emerging from the bathroom, and Sikorsky clubbed him over the head with the butt of his pistol. Nazif was stuffing something into his pocket, but on seeing the muzzle of my gun, dropped instantly to his knees and started yammering something in Turkish, his eyes wide and his hands clasped before him. He had dropped the thing he was putting into his pocket—Ari's pearls.

Fr. Jamie re-entered, throwing before him another Turk. Behind him, rubbing welts around his wrists where he had been bound, came Fritz.

"Fritz!" I cried. "Och, I'm glad to see you well."

"*Danke*, Herr McCracken," answered Fritz, his eyes leveled murderously on the two Turks who were still conscious.

Fr. Jamie looked down at the handsome Turk. "Ah, I see you've found young Kemal," he said. He tossed me some rope. "Tie their hands, laddie," he said, "then let's get them all down to the dining room and we can find out what they've been doing to our airship."

"Don't kill me, please!" cried Nazif. "He made us do it—he forced us!" He jabbed a stubby finger at the still-unconscious Kemal.

"You will kindly speak when you're spoken to, and not on any other occasions," I said, securing his hands behind his back. In the meantime, Fr. Jamie secured Kemal, who was groaning and beginning to come round. Fr. Jamie reached up, filled a glass with cold water, and dashed it in the Turk's face. The man woke up, spluttering.

"Aye, that's a little better, laddie," said Fr. Jamie. "Now, get on your feet and let's be having a wee conversation downstairs."

Fritz and Sikorsky steered a babbling Nazif and Turk Number Three out of the cabin and along the hallway, then down the steps to the main deck of the LS3 while Fr. Jamie and I held Kemal by the elbows and propelled him along behind them.

We had just reached the top of the steps when there came a woman's scream from outside, cut short abruptly.

Fear exploded in me. We had left Ari there.

Leaving the Turk with Fr. Jamie, I leaped down to the lower deck, making the Sign of the Cross as I went. A moment later, I clattered down the mobile steps to the hard ground of the aerodrome.

Ari was on the ground, a hand to her head; I could see a tiny smear of blood between her fingers. Of the two Turks she had been guarding, one was still unconscious, while the other had taken off and was dashing away at full speed, weaving as he went. He hadn't bothered to pick up Ari's Luger, which lay a couple of yards from her.

I dropped to my knee and leveled my revolver at the escaping Turk.

"*Mein Herr*," said Fritz's voice, "give me the gun."

The Turk was already twenty yards away, almost the extremity of the revolver's accurate range. I lined him up along the sight-blade, but he wove, and the shadows were dense, and I couldn't get a clear shot.

"*Mein Herr!*" insisted Fritz.

At this range, I could easily miss, or I could kill him, and that would be bad—all I wanted to do was bring him down.

The Turk dodged left, then right. Now he was out of the accurate range of the revolver, and I would have to trust to luck not to kill him. "Blessed Gabriel Possenti, guide my bullet," I said, and my finger tensed on the trigger.

A shot rang out beside me, and the Turk dropped.

I looked up, amazed. "Fritz!" I said. He was just beginning to lower the Luger. "I didn't know you were such a good shot."

Fritz glanced at me briefly. "There were in the service of the Baron von Helleher-Stauffen many opportunities to improve my marksmanship, Herr McCracken." He handed the Luger to Ari, who was getting shakily to her feet.

"What happened, my love?" I asked Ari.

"I was startled by a noise and turned my back for a moment," she said, "and he must have woken up."

"He hit you?" I said, prying her fingers from the wound on her forehead.

"He pushed me," she said, "and I hit my head on the mobile steps. It's not as bad as it looks—you know how foreheads bleed. I'm fine. You'd better see to that Turk. Is he dead, Fritz?"

"*Nein*, Frau McCracken," replied Fritz, a trace of wounded pride in his voice. "I aim for his leg."

Sure enough, as Fritz and I approached the Turk, we saw that he was writhing in pain, and we could hear his groans plainly. Fritz had got him just below the knee, and probably broken the bone, but it was nothing that wouldn't eventually heal. I marveled silently at Fritz's shot, and wondered how he had managed it, with his eyes that looked in different directions. Fritz and I pulled the Turk to his feet and helped him back towards the airship. He cursed and moaned all the way.

Fritz and Ari got him up the steps and into the gondola, while I shook his companion awake and pushed him after them. He didn't argue with my revolver, and we all proceeded quietly to the *Speiseraum*, where Sikorsky was ready with rope to bind the pair of them.

Fr. Jamie pulled a first-aid kit from under the bar, soused a swab with vodka (Sikorsky shaking his head at the waste as he did so) and washed and bound Ari's head wound. When he had finished, he turned to me.

"Cracky," he said, "a word, if you please."

We spent a few words in conversation outside the *Speiseraum*. Fr. Jamie had a plan he wanted to share with me. Then we went back in. Sikorsky had all five Turks tied up and was covering them with his revolver. Fritz had poured Ari a drink, and she was sitting on a stool at the bar, sipping it and staring impassively at the captives.

"Now," said Fr. Jamie, picking up a table, putting it onto its feet, and placing his revolver on it, "I think it's time you jessies did a wee bit of talking. What do you know about Babak Fort?"

"Father!" I cried out in a chiding voice.

"What?"

I took him aside, and said in a whisper, "They might not know about Babak Fort." But I noticed that Kemal had suddenly got a hungry look.

"Well, that's just fine," responded Fr. Jamie, turning back to the Turks. "We'll just drop them out of the airship over the desert, and have done with it."

The Turks writhed in fear and the wounded one cursed us in his language. Except Kemal. He watched us with derisive eyes, his lips turned down at the corners.

"Fritz," I said, "search these wallies."

Fritz and Ari moved over to the Turks. There followed a few moments while they searched their pockets and Fritz bandaged and splinted the wounded Turk's leg. The Turks complained bitterly while this was going on, except Kemal, who took it all with stoic indifference. We found they had pocketed some jewelry and cash they had located, but the manuscript wasn't among their plunder. Ari slipped out of the dining room.

"Well, my guess is that you failed to find what you were searching for," I said, "though you seem to have found plenty of other things that don't belong to you. Sikorsky, can you think of one reason why we don't just tip them out over the Caspian Sea?"

"No reason at all, McCracken." Sikorsky's mouth was turned down grimly at each corner.

"No, no, no, no, no!" pleaded Nazif. He was almost weeping with anguish. Kemal slowly turned his head and looked with contempt upon Nazif. Nazif said, "We tell you everything you need to know, McCracken Bey! Don't kill us! Don't hurt us!"

"There's nothing you can tell me that I wish to know," I replied. "I know who sent you—your boss, Kaiser Wilhelm. I know what you wanted. The only question before us is what to do with you."

"Kill us, then," said Kemal. "We go straight to *Jannah*. I welcome this prospect, *effendi*. Are you so certain that you will go directly to your Christian Heaven?"

"Kemal, what are you saying?" demanded Nazif, his voice rising in pitch. "Do not listen to him, honourable friends. He spends too much time with the Germans!"

Fritz slid back the safety on the Luger. "May I shoot him now, *mein Herr*?" he asked.

"Wait just a few minutes," I answered. "I don't want any more mess on the floor."

Kemal's nostrils flared. "You have no idea what you are facing, McCracken Bey. If you kill us, more will come. And more. And more. We are only the first, *effendi*. The Kaiser has many men, Turks and Germans. You cannot win—the numbers overwhelm. Kill us, set us free—it makes no difference.

For the Germans, it is but a matter of numbers. For us—" He leaned forward, and his handsome face became very fierce. "For us, this is *jihad*, the holy war. First, we destroy Britain and France, with the Kaiser's help, and then we destroy the Kaiser. The Crescent will rise over all, and the new era will begin—the era of Mohammed, prophet of the true God, the era of men of courage, the era of men of the true faith. Men who are not afraid to face death. Men destined for *Jannah*."

"Gardens of perpetual bliss," said Fr. Jamie, with a musing quality in his voice; we all turned to look at him. "They shall enter there, as well the righteous among their fathers, their spouses, and their children, and angels shall enter unto them from every gate, with the salutation, 'Peace unto ye, for that ye persevered in patience! Now how excellent is thy final home!'" He smiled.

Kemal looked at him with the beginnings of wonder in his eyes. "The western priest knows the Qu'ran?" he said.

"Aye, I do," responded Fr. Jamie. "But I know that also it is written, 'And the Lord God planted a garden in the east, and out of the ground He made to grow every tree that is pleasant to the sight and good for food.' Where your faith ends, *effendi*, mine begins."

"But I do not wish to see it now!" Nazif broke in. "Do not hurt us, *effendi*, and I will tell you what you need to know—what is in the eastern *yazisi*—the paper, the leaf."

Kemal said in a leisurely drawl, "Nazif, you are even more foolish than you are ugly. You know nothing of the contents of the eastern manuscript."

Oddly enough, I believed him when he said that, but Nazif insisted: "No, *effendi*—there is a distant land, full of lemon trees and rivers flowing with honey, and an abundance of kebabs, and where one can sleep long hours in the shade of trees, and there are many wives to be enjoyed, and—"

"You are a disgrace to all of us, Nazif," Kemal cut in.

"Well," said Fr. Jamie, "we can't let you go, so we'll just take you a very long way into the desert and leave you there." He turned to Fritz and Sikorsky. "Lock them into the end cabin on the port side," he said. "We'll deal with them later."

And amid protests and groans from four of the Turks and icy indifference from Kemal, Sikorsky and Fritz pushed them out of the *Speiseraum* and up the steps to the top deck.

CHAPTER 7
THE FORTRESS OF THE EAGLE'S EYE

At about two o'clock in the morning, Fr. Jamie and I sat in the dining room of the LS3, the lights off and the floor somewhat cleared of the debris left behind by the search. We had rescued a bottle of whisky from the wreckage, and were sipping from glasses meditatively, saying nothing, waiting. Something stirred in the doorway, and we saw that Sikorsky had appeared.

"McCracken," he said, "Fr. Jamie, I think Turks have escaped."

"How do you know?" I asked.

"I hear them whisper together through door. I cannot understand Turkish, and they know it. But I guess what they say. Then I hear nothing for a while, then some quiet moving around, then nothing again."

"There they are," said Fr. Jamie, pointing through the window. Sure enough, four figures were moving across the airfield, snatching furtive glances over their shoulders. "I suppose they left their wounded man behind."

"I hope they haven't killed him," I said. "We'd better go and check."

We opened the door of the cabin briefly and looked in. The Turk inside grinned menacingly and said, "My friends, they escape. You cannot keep them here!"

"I most certainly hope they did escape," replied Fr. Jamie, closing the door without glancing back at the Turk's crestfallen face. "Vasili Ivanovich," he said, "you'd better make sure *he* doesn't escape, or else he'll tell them their escape was all part of our plan."

Sikorsky nodded and went into the cabin to secure the porthole. We knew that the porthole of that cabin had a loose frame, and I'd been meaning to fix it since we left France, but hadn't got around to it; now I was glad I'd been so neglectful. Sikorsky tightened a few screws, and Fr. Jamie and I left him to his work.

"Two hundred miles on camel and horse," said Fr. Jamie, "across the desert. That will take them about a week. We can get to Babak Fort in about half a day's flying, and be well ahead of them, hiding."

"It'll be quite a job to hide the LS3," I pointed out. "Perhaps in a nearby valley?"

"So long as we're all out of sight when they turn up—if they even catch a hint we're there, they won't reveal the clue they have."

One of the cabin doors clicked, and Ari emerged. She had thrown a dressing gown about her shoulders and was tightening the belt. She still had some sticking-plaster on her forehead. "Did they get away?" she asked. I nodded. "Great," she went on. "Now we can find out what their half of the manuscript says."

The LS3 rose into the air just when the sun rose over the Caspian Sea, kindling a fire more beautiful by far than those that wavered atop the oil derricks. Baku vanished slowly behind us, and we hastened over the rocky desert, which rose to bare, mountainous peaks. I divided my time between the *Speiseraum*, which Ari and I set about cleaning, and the navigation room, where I plotted our course and shouted our headings through the doorway to Sikorsky, who was at the wheel.

We had made a lot of progress on the *Speiseraum*, when Fr. Jamie hurried in with a message from Sikorsky.

"It looks like we've arrived," he announced.

I glanced at my watch as we hurried forward—it wasn't even noon. I smiled to think of the trouble Kemal and Nazif would be having getting the animals together while we were exploring leisurely and finding the best vantage points from which to spy upon them when they arrived. I longed for them to find a quicker way of getting to Babak Fort. But it looked like we were in for one of those boring parts of adventures—the long waiting that makes up such a large portion of the adventurous life.

When we got to the wheel-house, we found that Sikorsky had reduced speed and we were cruising up to the fort. It was perched on the top of a vertiginous cliff, surrounded by ragged mountains, most of which were covered with sparse grass and a few trees. It had once been a mighty fortress, but time had eroded its walls, which were crumbling and uneven. We could clearly see its plan as we flew over—an upper fort comprising a wide courtyard and a few small buildings, and a lower fort connected to it by wide steps, where the courtyard was narrower and the buildings larger. Most of them were open to the sky, though a few were sheltered by the remnants of roofs.

"I'll get the radios," said Ari, disappearing from the wheel-house. I went aft, and slung my pack over my shoulder. In a moment, Ari had joined me, shouldering her own backpack.

Sikorsky brought the LS3 down to within a few feet of the top courtyard of the castle, and Ari and I climbed down the rope-ladder. When she touched the ground, Ari spoke into the radio: "Okay, Vasili. We'll call you when we need to be picked up."

"*Da*," answered Sikorsky's voice over the radio. "We see you soon."

Fritz hauled on the rope ladder, which retracted, swinging wildly, into the gondola. Then the engines revved up, and the LS3 turned away from the fort.

We stood in the middle of a wide yard, about thirty feet by sixty or so, the ground hard-packed dust beneath our feet. The walls were about twice my height, but the wall at the north end was taller, and ragged at the top.

"This wasn't originally a courtyard," Ari observed. "Look at those projections near the top of the north wall: the floor of an upper story originally rested on those. This was the keep."

"Mm-hm," I said, moving towards the eastern wall, where the stone had crumbled away almost to the ground for about a dozen feet. It looked as if a big bite had been taken out of it. Through it, we could see yellowish mountains, the lower slopes clad with thick trees. Left and right, the castle spilled down the slopes like a mangle-wheel, the different parts connected by long flights of steps.

"Look at this," said Ari, moving over to the east wall eight or ten feet from the breach.

"What do you see?" I asked.

She pointed. "Doesn't that look like an eagle's head?" she asked.

I squinted and cocked my head on one side. "I don't see it," I said.

She traced the beak with her slender forefinger, and then jabbed at a hole that went all the way through the wall. "That's its eye," she concluded. "It's an eagle's head, with a hole through the wall for its eye. I wonder why they would carve that?" She looked around. "I don't see any other kind of decoration."

"You have a vivid imagination," I said.

"I guess," Ari said slowly, "eagles were important to the Khoramdin. You can see why, building their strongholds in places like this."

"Mm-hm," I said again. Turning away from the Eagle's Head, I suggested, "We'd better get familiar with this place. When Kemal and his chums get here, we'll need to find a lot of places to hide."

We left the keep and took some steps into a lower court. A maze of walls of differing heights showed where the castle's inhabitants had once lived. One of the buildings was still topped by a roof. A pair of wide windows looked out from a second story. Below this, an arched doorway led onto a wide walkway where the sentries would presumably have paced.

"No need to fear much from attack, though," Ari pointed out. "Not many armies could have attacked up these slopes."

"The more interesting question," I said, "is how they got workmen up here to build it, and materials." I peeped over the wall, and saw that, below the vertical sides of the cliff lay a pile of loose stones reaching halfway up the peak's height. "Well, there's the stone," I said, "and they got the wood from the forest over there, but it's still quite a climb with all that heavy stuff. You have to admire them."

But before Ari could reply, I held up my hand in warning.

"What is it?" asked Ari in a whisper.

I scanned the horizon, and at last saw what I was looking for: a black dot, perhaps a finger's width above the mountain-tops to the north-west.

"That's an aeroplane," I said. "Let's hide."

It wasn't difficult to get inside the fort and find an arrow-loop through which we could observe the newcomer. It was still nothing much more than a flattened dot, but I could hear the sound of its engine plainly.

"That's a Mercedes engine," I said, "about a hundred horsepower."

"What does that mean?" wondered Ari.

"Well, it's an engine that's used in a variety of aeroplanes, all German in manufacture." I listened for a moment. "It's a single-engined aircraft, so it's not a G1. It's either an Albatross B1 or an Aviatik B1, unless they're using them in other planes by now. They're both twin-seaters." I looked through the arrow-loop again, and now the plane was close enough that I could see red and white roundels on the wings and a crescent moon and a star on the tail-plane. "Yes," I said, "it looks as if Kemal's been able to borrow an Albatross B1 from the Turkish Air Force."

There was nowhere on the summit of the hill to land an aeroplane, but Ari and I watched from behind the wall of the walkway as the Albatross landed in the valley below. We had plenty of time to scout out places to hide as two tiny figures climbed out of the plane, far below, and began their arduous trek up the side of the cliff to the fortress of the ancient freedom fighters.

I had expected that we would have about a week before Kemal and the others caught up with us here. I had not reckoned on his being able to get a plane from the Turkish Air Force. Part of me was impressed, very impressed—another part was relieved that we wouldn't have quite so long to wait. Most of all, I was glad that we had moved so quickly, without waiting to take on new supplies. If we had delayed by even a couple of hours, we might have missed him, and so missed the clue he was going to give us unwittingly. Providence again, I thought.

The steps leading up to Babak Fort wound this way and that up the sheer cliff, and the two figures were often out of sight. I could see, before long, that Kemal was indeed one of them men who had arrived in the plane; the other was unknown to me—presumably the pilot. He had removed his leather flying jacket and slung it over his shoulder. It was not particularly hot—the elevation and the season made it cooler than you would expect—but they were exerting themselves as they laboured up.

I found a place to conceal myself and eavesdrop, on top of a wall. It was a wide wall, and I could hide by lying flat. To my left was the lower courtyard, to my right a short drop to the bare mountainside, where a narrow shelf of rock ran along the wall. So at any time, I could let myself down onto that little ledge and move back and forth, up to the upper courtyard and back, with some freedom. Ari found a similar hiding place on the opposite side of the fort, and I hoped she'd see and hear more than me—without knowing Turkish, I wasn't confident I could understand what was going on.

Kemal and the pilot reached the summit of the mountain. The pilot sat down and said something to Kemal, fanning himself with a sheaf of papers. Kemal replied in Turkish and strode away from him. He walked through each room, casting his eye over all the walls as he went. He passed by me, and started climbing the steps to the upper courtyard.

I slipped down to the narrow ledge on the cliffside, and inched towards the top fort. With a little effort, I could place myself on the outside of the east wall of the upper courtyard. At my back stood the green and yellow mountains; the rock under my hands and pressed against my chest was uneven and rough.

I heard Kemal enter the upper courtyard. His feet crunched on the loose dirt as he walked from one end to the other.

Another noise: the pilot had arrived. He spoke to Kemal, who replied. They were moving towards the east wall, the wall with the wide breach in it, and me behind it.

Kemal shouted to the pilot, and together they hurried to the wall. Through the breach, I could just see Kemal as he moved close to the wall and put his eye to it. I flattened myself against the wall, against the floor, as much as I could. Kemal and the pilot chattered to one another incomprehensibly. Kemal stepped back from the wall, and the pilot put his eye to it.

I remembered the hole in the wall that made the eye in the eagle's head, and realized that they were looking through that.

Kemal and the pilot talked some more, and disappeared from the wall. I edged nearer to the breach, and peered cautiously through it. They were looking at something spread out on the ground between them—a map, I guessed, and remembered the sheaf of papers with which the pilot had been fanning himself. But I caught only a quick glimpse of what was going on; it wasn't safe to look for very long.

On the further side of the breach, I saw a movement, and looked up. Ari had left her hiding place on the further side of the fortress and joined me here, on the east side. But she couldn't get any closer to me without exposing herself to their view. Hitting upon an idea, she found the eye of the carved eagle from the outside, and peered through its eye from her side. But no sooner had she placed her eye against the eagle's than she jerked back suddenly because the pilot had got up to look through it one more time. I flattened myself against the wall, hardly daring to breathe. But he didn't look in my direction. He looked through the eagle's eye, consulted his map, marked something on it, and then returned to Kemal. They spoke together again, but now their voices were receding as they walked out of the upper courtyard and back towards the fort's exit.

Ari and I peered through the breach to make sure no one was there, and then entered the courtyard once more.

"Did you understand any of that?" I asked in a stage whisper.

"Shshhh!" she hissed, laying a finger to her lips. Crossing the courtyard quickly and nimbly, she looked down the steps. I stood behind her. We could see Kemal and the pilot, their backs to us. In a moment, they had passed through the exit and begun their descent to the valley floor.

Ari whirled round to face me. "They were looking for something called the Eye of the Eagle. It's part of what we were looking at before—the eagle's head we found. They were looking through the Eye, and at a map."

"Probably getting a bearing," I said. We both returned to the far end of the courtyard, where the image of the eagle glared at us out of the stone. I peered through. In the middle of the aperture I could see a peak, taller than the others. It would have had a sharp summit, except that the top widened out slightly and flattened. It looked like a bowl or a cup perched precariously up there on top of a rocky needle.

"Their clue was that the Eagle's Eye would show them the Nest," said Ari, "and that they would then have the bearing for the Tower of Babel."

I smiled as suddenly I understood. "Well, there's the Nest," I said, standing aside so that Ari could look through the Eye. "That rock on top of the peak—it looks exactly like a nest."

Ari stared for a moment, then straightened up, smiling. "Can you calculate the heading?" she asked.

"Can the Pope pray Grace?" I retorted, pulling my compass out of my pocket. I flipped the case open and lined it up with the hole. Looking from the compass-face to the Eagle's Nest and back again, I said, "115 degrees."

"115 degrees what?" asked Ari. "East? North? Northeast?"

"Degrees, dear," I said, kissing her on the nose. "Degrees are always measured from North. There are 360 of them altogether. 115 degrees is roughly east-southeast."

The distant sound of a Mercedes engine rose to us from the valley floor, and we looked out together through the breach in the wall as the Albatross B1 soared up into the sky and headed off towards Baku again.

"We're only a little ahead of them," I said, a little sadly.

"Perhaps more than that," said Ari. "They were talking about their whole journey. They spoke of the Silk Road, explored by Marco Polo, and a place east of Babel called Monday-City."

"The Silk Road," I said. "Monday-City is one of the clues we have. Was there anything else?"

"Something about a Stony River, where fish are found, and going across a wide desert."

"We need to see a map," I said.

Ari nodded, taking out her radio to call Sikorsky. I could still see the Albatross silhouetted against the pale sky, and I watched it vanish from sight. Ari slipped her arm through mine. "So," she said, "a heading of 115 degrees takes us to the Tower of Babel; we go east to Monday-City. Near there is a Sea of Rocks and a Stony River. There are fish, but there's no water. We follow the Stony River to a wide desert."

"Then comes the big problem," I said, "the difficult clue. Sunrise in the west. I'm not such a fool as to think that the sun rises *due* east, but I know it never rises in the west. There has to be something else in the clue, but what? Didn't you hear anything else?"

86

There must have been a note of irritation in my voice, because Ari dropped my arm and looked at me with pursed lips, as if she'd bitten into a lemon. "There's a solution," she told me earnestly. "Obviously that meant something to Prester John and Pero da Covilha."

"But it doesn't make any sense," I protested. "There can't be any place in the world where the earth starts rotating the other way."

"Remember what Sherlock Holmes says," answered Ari. "First, eliminate the impossible. Then, whatever remains must be the solution."

"All right," I said, "let's eliminate the impossible. The sun can't rise in the west. What's left? Nothing!"

"O ye of little faith," chided Ari. "It only *seems* impossible. There's one place on earth where such a clue makes sense. All the world isn't an engineering problem. There are more things in heaven and earth, Mac, than are dreamt of in your philosophy."

"Is that all you can do?" I inquired pointedly. "Quote Shakespeare and Sir Arthur Conan Doyle at me?"

"*O ye of little faith* is from the Bible," countered Ari. "But when our brains fail, it's as well to go to those who are smarter. All I really mean is that some things happen that science can't explain."

"Or can't explain *yet*," I replied.

"Or maybe it never will. In some ways, the most important things that happen can't be easily explained. How can a man die and rise again in three days?"

I struggled to put into words what my objections were. Slowly, I said, "Ari, science is predictable. We try to construct rules that happen every time certain circumstances are fulfilled. Drop an object, and gravity will always pull it towards the ground. We don't deny miracles; we just recognize them as unique. But since they're unique, you can't use them for directions getting any place—the sun won't rise in the west by miracle every time some Zunian wants to get back home."

Ari sighed. "Then there has to be a natural explanation for it, but you'll have to wait to find out what it is," she said. "Either way, you have to have faith."

I drew in a deep breath. The wind was beginning to blow coolly out of the north. "If you insist," I said. "I'll just stop thinking about it and see what happens."

A moment later, we heard the engines of the LS3, and the rope-ladder was unfurling for us. I hastened to the wheel-house to give Sikorsky the heading, and before we could have reasonably reckoned on it, we were underway.

"Mac!" came Ari's voice from the navigation room. She had a map of Russia and Afghanistan spread out on the table before her.

"What have you found, love?" I asked.

She pointed. And there, about 350 miles away from Babak Fort, and precisely at a heading of 115 degrees, was a city named Babol.

CHAPTER 8

SUNRISE IN THE WEST

W e stopped in Baku towards nightfall to refuel. For a couple of hours, Sikorsky and I stood on the gantries beside the fuel intakes, while the snakelike hoses twitched like live things, disgorging their petroleum into the LS3's tanks. The fires of Baku were lit all around us, but I tried not to look at them. I felt a little ashamed, in truth.

We were underway again as the sun rose. I stood beside Sikorsky in the wheel-house, and watched the sun peer over the verdant slopes of the mountains ahead of us, casting gold into the Caspian Sea on our port, and throwing long shadows like black spears towards us.

"I thought all this part of the world was desert," I said.

"No, is very beautiful," replied Sikorsky. "Legends say, this is where our first parents lived in Eden."

The bottom edge of the sun parted company with the mountain-tops, and the crimson and gold layers in the clouds subdued themselves to purple and then to blue and white. The day had begun.

It was mid-morning when we approached the city of Babol. The forest that covered most of the mountains approached the city closely, so that in its autumnal colours, the city seemed to be wrought from gold, encrusted here and there with rubies.

Setting down in a park in the middle of the city, we found a bazaar that consisted of some makeshift stalls set up in the middle of a square, not much more than blankets tied to a wall and propped up on the other side with tall poles. Under the awnings, oranges were for sale, and lemons and limes; there was roast lamb gently spiced, with piles of steaming couscous; lamps, knives and samovars of brass, jewelry boxes and small tables of aromatic wood; silks like rainbows spread out over the tables, and loose or in vessels of copper, stone, or glass, all manner of nuts, spices, and perfumes.

Ari gravitated towards one of the silk merchants, and I hung back, disapproving of the unnecessary expenditure. But when she came back, with green and purple silks draped over her arm, she told us what she had discovered: the city of Dyushambe, in Tajikistan, was due east of Babol, and had from time out of mind supported a market every Monday. We returned to the LS3 and spent the rest of the day re-provisioning.

By the evening, Babol was bright with golden lights shining from thousands of windows, but one particularly tall building arrested my attention as I stood surveying the city from the panoramic windows in the *Speiseraum*. It dominated the skyline, a great cubic structure with spindly columns supporting a flat roof on one side.

"I could almost imagine that the Tower of Babel," I remarked, pointing it out to Ari.

"That's the palace of Shah Abbas the Great," Ari said, as if it was a fact everyone knew. "It's far too late for the Tower of Babel—the Shah built it in the sixteenth century. But a legend goes that he built it there because it was on the site of the Tower of Babel; he built it one ell shorter than the Tower so as not to offend Allah."

"What's an ell?"

"The length of an arrow," she replied, "about forty inches."

"Hm," I grunted. "Perhaps he just couldn't get an architect good enough to go up to the full height."

We rose with the sun, pointed the LS3's nose into the east and began once more our voyage. Dyushambe was a two-day trip, but we had enough fuel, so we landed in the middle of nowhere to sleep, rising early the following morning for Mass, breakfast, and a flight into the sunrise. Sikorsky, Fritz and I took turns at the wheel. As often as not, Fr. Jamie would stand beside the helmsman, staring into the distance with anticipation or praying the rosary. His eye was always on the land ahead, eager to pick out a detail here or there.

It was in the evening during that part of the trip, when we were all enjoying drinks in the dining room, and the world was turning purple all about us, when Sikorsky asked, "Fr. Jamie, I am curious. Why do you have interest in Prester John's Land? Where is it you get your knowledge?"

"Och, laddie," Fr. Jamie replied, setting down his glass of rum, "there's a long, long answer to that question. But I reckon the best one is that I'm curious to see the land that was evangelized by St. Thomas the Apostle. Doubting Thomas, he's often called, though I think that's a little unfair. I think most of us feel a kind of fellowship with St. Thomas—the one who doubted Our Lord's resurrection until he put his hands inside Our Lord's wounds. Most of us doubt what we cannot see."

"Like a place where the sunrise is in the west," said Ari, nudging me with her elbow.

"That's one that might occasion some doubt indeed," replied Fr. Jamie. "But I dinna hold with calling the poor Saint Doubting Thomas. I prefer to call him Faithful Thomas. I suspect that after his incident with Our Lord's wounds, Doubting Thomas never doubted again. If you told Doubting Thomas, 'One day, you'll find a land where the sun rises in the west,' he'd no doubt say, 'I doubt it not. That will be the Land of Eternal Life.'"

"Or the Land of Zun," I added.

"Well, no doubt there'll be an explanation for that, Cracky," Fr. Jamie told me, holding his glass up in a kind of toast. He reflected for a moment, then went on, "The other reason I'm curious about the Land of Zun is, it's a place where the Faith is pure. They've had no contact with the outside world, save one excursion at the time of the Crusades, since the time of the Apostle. So you realize what that means?" He looked round at each one of us in turn, and his eye glinted with the last rays of the sun outside the gondola. "Can you imagine the Faith, if it never had to deal with the Black Death, with the Great Schism? And more important, a faith untrammeled by the Reformation and the filth and exploitation of the Industrial Revolution? Think about that. All the factories, the steam engines, the iron, the banks, where have they led us? Thousands of boys sitting in the mud in Belgium, shooting at other boys sitting in the mud a few yards away—boys they couldn't tell from Adam, but with whom they'd probably share a beer or a cigarette if ever they met. It's an inhuman world we've created, my dears, and I'd dearly love to see what it could have been like. Perhaps in Zun is the solution to our world's great problems."

I had felt the hairs prickle on the back of my neck as he had spoken; but I also felt compelled to defend some industry. "There's nothing wrong with steam engines and iron," I said, almost apologetically. "Look at the Clifton Suspension Bridge or the Rocket. Isambard Kingdom Brunel and George Stephenson were artists as well as industrialists. Industry doesn't have to be ugly."

"No, it disna," replied Fr. Jamie, "but it often is. Men can make steam engines and bridges beautiful, but they'd mostly rather make them cheap, and it's too easy to make profit your only motive. Love the machine, Cracky, but hate the factory."

"Evil is in man," commented Sikorsky, "not in machine."

"It's a fallen world," commented Ari. But then her features took on a new aspect, and she leaned forward, setting her almost empty champagne glass on the table. "I wonder," she said, "why the people of Zun never emerged from their lost valley? Did a plague wipe them all out, perhaps? Did they have a series of bad rulers?"

Fr. Jamie drained his glass and set it down on the table, stretching his huge limbs at he rose from his chair. "There are many mysteries," he said, "that I hope will be solved by our little expedition. I pray to the Almighty that the Zunians won't all be long dead when we get there. Well, I'm for bed, my dears. I'll see you all in the morning."

I was at the helm the following afternoon, when we came up on Dyushambe. It wasn't much more than a village at the confluence of two rivers, beyond which rose a range of mountains, their peaks already shrouded in early snows. At the feet of the mountains, and stretching out into the south, was a wide and rocky desert, the light glancing from its surface like white-caps on a choppy sea.

"There's Monday-City," I observed, as Sikorsky entered to take the wheel. "Where do we go now?"

"Sea of Rocks and Stony River, where are fish," said Sikorsky drily.

"Well, that's a Sea of Rocks if ever I saw one," I said, throwing the wheel about so that we began to cruise over the rocky ground of the desert south of Dyushambe.

The Sea of Rocks—if it was truly that—was not wide, and was fringed to the south by another mountain range, yellow and bare. We moored the LS3, and began our search for the Stony River the next morning.

As it turned out, we had no need of a lengthy search. An hour after we had taken to the air, Sikorsky called us all to the wheel-house, and pointed out of the port windows. We all peered through them, and saw what he had seen: strange shapes in the hillside, too regular for nature, which seemed to have been carved into fish-shapes.

Not too regular for nature, I realized with a start: they were fossilized fish, set into the rocks of the hillside. I could see ranks upon ranks of ribs, monstrous jaws, curved tails, occasionally a fin. They seemed to flip and curvette out of the stone wall, slip around each other, dart and dance and dodge as the shadow of the LS3 flitted over them.

And then, at precisely the point where the fish gathered most closely, there was a cleft in the mountains—a gorge, leading southwards. Sikorsky turned the wheel, and we curved in among the mountains. The Stony River was all yellow rocks, with no vegetation whatever. But it had certainly once been part of an inland sea, for the fossilized sea creatures were everywhere, and easily visible from the gondola, as we flew close to the ground.

Soon, the fossilized creatures grew fewer, and then there were no more. But the valley went on for mile after unchanging mile. Occasionally, we saw a great bird of prey, its wings outspread, turning on the air currents, and I wondered what on earth it could find to eat in such a barren wilderness. Before long, most of us lost interest, and wandered off to other pursuits.

All except Fr. Jamie, who stood beside Sikorsky the whole way, his eyes gleaming as he turned his head this way and that.

At about noon, we found ourselves emerging from the Stony River and looking out over a wide, flat, yellow expanse—a great desert.

"Zun lies across a wide desert," observed Ari, reconstructing the conversation between Kemal and the pilot in her memory. "There, we'll find the place where the sunrise is in the west."

In the navigation room, I took out the map. There was Dyushambe, there the mountains we had crossed, there the desert.

"There's another mountain range," I said, "about eighty miles south."

"We should reach before nightfall," said Sikorsky.

"Zun was supposed to be a valley," said Fr. Jamie, almost to himself. "But where, amongst those mountains?"

"Sunrise in the west," said Ari brightly, as if that explained everything.

"McCracken," said Sikorsky, when we were underway once more, "Number 3 engine has low RPM." He pointed at one of the dials.

"Probably just a sticky prop," I said, "but I'll take a look."

I crawled out of one of the maintenance hatches and onto one of the exterior gantries that ran along the top of the gondola. Walking along it, holding tight to the guide-rail, I could see into each of the cabins along the way. On the other side was the desert, wider and flatter than my mind could properly understand. The wind was terrific out there, flattening my shirt against my back as I made my way to the sternmost port-side engine.

The low RPMs were often caused by what's called a sticky prop. Sometimes, when an engine's being overhauled, as the LS3's had been recently, the crew will tighten the blade bearings a bit too much and cause the prop to catch slightly. That shows up in a multi-engine aircraft as low RPMs. Sikorsky had shut off both rear engines, and I went to work with my spanner for a few minutes. When I had finished, I put my tools back into the box and began my return to the maintenance hatch.

Ahead of us, I could now see a long line of blue mountains, capped with snow, on the horizon. I stopped a moment to contemplate them, the wind whistling through the gantry and the wires. I wondered where beyond that thin blue line the Land of Zun could be located, and how the impenetrable clue of sunrise in the west could possibly be interpreted. The mountains didn't offer any answer; they didn't even seem to get any closer.

But less than an hour later, we had arrived.

They rose out of the desert floor without any foothills, sheer and grey, like jagged sheets of steel. They stretched out in a ragged line east and west, diminishing to nothing at the horizon.

"Which way we go?" asked Sikorsky.

"Let's try west," I said, and looking across at Ari, added, "where the sun rises."

Sikorsky threw over the helm, and we turned to the starboard. The snow-capped peaks gazed down on us, almost as if mocking us. The sun began to decline—to set into the west, not rise from it—and we set down the airship in the shelter of an arm of mountains. They were all covered with snow, and opposite them, in the east, was a series of low hills, so that we rested in a shallow, broad valley whose sides were of unequal height.

We all retired in a despondent mood, resolved to rise early and recommence our fruitless search.

I slept poorly, and waking at five o'clock in the morning, went down to the galley, fried myself a couple of eggs and brewed some coffee. In the dining room, I wolfed down the eggs and sipped at the coffee, poring over the inscrutable manuscript. There had to be another clue, I reasoned.

Out of the windows, the sun rose, the soft crimson glow coming through the windows on the port side.

Suddenly, my eyes grew wide. The port side faced west.

Slowly, my heart beating almost audibly, I rose from my table and stared at what was happening outside.

The sun had not risen yet. It was still hidden behind the low hills in the east. But it shone its crimson light past those hills and onto the snow-clad mountain peaks in the west, bathing them all in its ruddy glow. In Europe, I knew, they called this phenomenon Alpenglow.

In the Land of Zun, they called it seeing sunrise in the west.

CHAPTER 9
COMBAT IN THE SKIES

No one doubted me about the sunrise in the west, even though nobody else saw it—it was gone before I could get to the upper deck and rouse everyone from their slumbers. I was the Doubting Thomas, after all, now faithful and docile. After a half hour's flurry of activity, Sikorsky throttled up the LS3 and the airship rose majestically into the air. The mountains slid downwards, and the peaks, laden with the first white of winter, appeared through the forward windows in the wheel-house.

Fritz bustled in, accompanied by a delectable smell of freshly-baked bread. "Breakfast is served," he said, "in the *Steuerraum*." He set up a table of veritable delights: fresh bread rolls, salami and ham, marmalade, honey, and chocolate spread, and a large carafe of fresh coffee, with cream and brown sugar. Our attention was, frankly, divided: a hitherto undiscovered utopia, or Fritz's breakfast. Fritz's breakfast won.

As my teeth sank through the soft, piping hot bread, the honey melting through the holes, I watched the mountain peaks pointing at us, the gondola almost bushing their fingertips. I poured a second cup of coffee, as a wide valley unfolded itself below.

There were at first no signs of inhabitants. A river issued from the side of one of the mountains over which we had passed. Its course was blue as oiled steel, as it cut through a steep gorge, grassy shelves on one side, deeply forested slopes on the other. We passed over a beaver's dam, regulating the water-flow into an inlet, and then over one wide shelf on the eastern side of the river.

That was where we saw our first Zunian. His house was built in the fold of land under a cliff, and he was standing outside it, a scythe in his hand. He looked up at us as we passed, a hand shielding his eyes.

Soon, we had left the gorge behind, and flew over wide pastures, deep green in colour, the river snaking left and right through the middle, the mountains grey and white on either side. Sometimes, a strip or a square of gold revealed a different crop, sometimes a field was peppered with beasts—ruddy little cattle or horses charging, rolling, or sunning themselves. Here, homesteads were scattered among the fields, the thatched roofs a shining brown in the early morning sun. We saw no villages, but the farms were all close enough to be easy walking distance from one another. The Zunians seemed to help one another out with the harvest, for the folk would congregate in one field, their scythes swishing

102

back and forth, the women gleaning and raking behind them. As we passed over one group, they all stopped their work to gaze, pointing, up at us.

We flew along a straight course, but occasionally the sides of the valley would turn in towards us, and we got a closer glimpse of the foothills, thickly forested with firs and birches. There was some pasture on the slopes too, but here the houses were different, more like huge tents, or *yurts*, as Ari called them, and here the fields were for the most part sprinkled with white dots—shepherding was apparently the major agriculture on the mountain slopes.

We picked up the river again not long afterwards. Birches and willows clustered about its banks, and every now and then we would see a house. One of them was evidently a mill—it had a tiled roof, and the wheel moved lazily in the river's even current.

"This is idyllic," I observed.

"It's strange that we haven't seen a large structure or a village yet," Ari answered. "You'd expect manor houses, like in medieval England or France, but we haven't seen anything yet to indicate any sort of social hierarchy. Everyone is a farmer, everyone has his own plot of land, it seems."

"If they've had no contact with the outside world for four centuries," reasoned Fr. Jamie, "they might have no need for defence."

"Manor houses were not just for defence," replied Ari. "They were administrative centres, they collected rents and taxes."

"You'll surely not be complaining about a lack of taxation, now, will you, my dear?" Fr. Jamie chided her gently.

Ari smiled. "Of course not," she said. "I'm just marveling at it, and I don't see right now how their society is organized. Pero da Covilha was Duke of Guzelvadi here; what does the term *duke* mean to the Zunians?"

No one had an answer to that, so we fell silent and watched the fields spread out below us, until Sikorsky caught sight of something new.

"Look," he said, pointing, "is dam!"

And indeed, that's what it was: a pale line stretching from one side of the valley to the other, at the base of which had collected a wide pool of water. I could just glimpse water, foaming through four evenly-spaced sluice-gates at the eastern end. Excitedly, I grabbed some of Fritz's Black Forest cake and returned to my aerial tour of Zun.

But then I caught something out of the corner of my eye. I stepped aft a little, craning forward to see more clearly.

Something in the air seemed to be following us, something I thought at first was a bird. When I looked again, though, I saw it was not a bird at all.

It was an aeroplane: an Albatross B1.

"Look out, everyone!" I cried. "Kemal's here!"

We all stared out of the starboard windows. The Albatross was closing in on us, and I could see two figures, the pilot in front and Kemal behind. Kemal was holding something long and straight and stick-like, which he was swinging around towards us.

My blood turned to ice. He had mounted a machine-gun in the rear cockpit of the Albatross.

"Get on the floor!" I yelled, and we all dived, just at the moment when the machine-gun opened up. Over our heads, glass shattered noisily. Fragments of it tinkled on the floor all around us. I heard bullets smack into the bulkheads behind us. Quickly, I put an arm around Ari, pulling her close to me for protection. The noise of the Mercedes engine came to us through the shattered windows, and we heard it pass us and fly on ahead. Stillness settled on the wheel-house; the noise of the LS3's engines seemed remote. Slowly, we all stood up.

"Anyone hurt?"

"Just breakfast," said Ari bitterly.

"I will get guns," said Fritz, his lips set grimly, "*und* ammunition."

A thousand yards ahead of us, the Albatross banked right, then curved round and swung in for another run. I felt my heart sink: how could we hope to escape injury this time? I wondered.

"Everybody," I said, "get out of the wheel-house until he's passed by."

Sikorsky lashed the wheel, and we all piled into the passageway. Hardly had we done so, when the machine-gun barked again, and we could hear shattering glass and a thump-thump-thump as bullets crashed into the gondola and the envelope.

The envelope! I thought. The hydrogen! I looked across at Sikorsky.

"Is no problem," said Sikorsky, reading my mind. "Hydrogen will not ignite—these bullets have low calibre. To pierce envelope, you need explosive rounds, to ignite hydrogen, you need incendiary rounds. Is not possible."

The airship lurched, as a bullet landed particularly heavily over our heads.

"We are safe," Sikorsky reassured us.

"Safe?" I pointed to a bullet-hole in the wall about an inch from my head.

"Relatively speaking," said Sikorsky.

Fritz was back now, and handing out revolvers, which we hurriedly loaded. Fritz kept the Luger for himself—old habits died hard with him, I guessed.

"Vasili," said Fr. Jamie, "I think you need to be at the wheel when you can be. Cracky, you and Ari in the wheel-house, Fritz and I in the dining room. That's the best way to get the best shots at this wally all through his attack run. We'll make him think twice each time he wants to take a shot at us!"

We scattered to our various posts, just as we heard the rattle of the machine gun begin again. I

106

found a spot in the wheel-house where I was relatively sheltered, but where a broken window gave me a clear field of fire. I leaned out of the window, just as the Albatross passed, and fired—six rounds in rapid succession. To my left, Ari opened up. I thought I saw some rents open up in the canvas fuselage, but no more damage than that. The Albatross banked, turned, and began a new attack-run.

Sikorsky was muttering something rapid in Russian.

"What is it, Vasili?" asked Ari.

"Dirigible will not climb," replied Sikorsky.

"Have they hit one of the elevators?" I wondered, crossing to the port side of the wheel-house.

"No, they still move. It is as if—" He broke off. "*Bozhe moi!*" he cried. "I think they may have punctured a ballonet. I must check."

"Is there danger from our gun-flashes?" asked Ari, reloading her revolver.

"*Nyet,*" answered Sikorsky, lashing the wheel again. "Hydrogen, it go up."

Ari sniffed the air. "What does hydrogen smell like?" she asked.

"It's odourless," I replied.

"Great," she said. "Then we wouldn't know anything until we were incinerated."

"Sikorsky says it rises," I countered, "and it does. Who's the one without faith now?"

"Watch out!" shouted Ari. "Here he comes again!"

I leveled my revolver as the Albatross roared up alongside. I could see Kemal's moustache above his gritted teeth, and the muzzle of the gun, flashing as the bullets exploded from it. The wheel-house was riddled with bullets, glass shattering and wood splintering. I fired off all six rounds, Ari doing the same beside me. I saw one wing-strut splinter—a lucky hit. But the plane sped on towards the stern of the airship, where we heard Fr. Jamie and Fritz open fire. I leaned out of the window to watch what would happen.

As I did so, the airship gave a lurch and tilted forward. Through the forward windows, we could see the shining waters of the reservoir.

I dashed over to the wheel, unlashed it and opened up the throttle.

Number 3 engine—the one I had fixed earlier—was losing power. One of the lines had probably taken a bullet.

At that moment, Sikorsky flew back into the wheel-house, and I reported what had happened to him.

"*Da*," he said. "These animals, they have ruptured ballonet. Hydrogen, it escape through holes in envelope." He crossed himself. "Thank God," he said, "they have no incendiary bullets. But we will lose altitude."

"I'll get out there and fix the engine, if I can," I said. As I dashed from the wheel-house, I heard the roar of the Mercedes engine and gunfire from Fr. Jamie and Fritz. The machine-gun opened up and the gondola lurched under the repeated hammer-blows.

I thrust a few tools into my belt and emerged on the port gantry of the LS3. The airship's nose was tilted downwards, and the gantry sloped up before my feet. I grasped the railing and pulled myself along the gantry, leaning forward for balance. It was like climbing a hill to get to the stern engine. The air rushed all around me, the three good engines roared; Number 3 was slowing, and oil was streaked along the envelope behind it. Sure enough, one of the lines had a nick in it from a near miss. It should be an easy fix, I thought, reaching for my spanner.

But then, from behind me, came a new noise: the Albatross was returning. With the beginnings of irritation, I turned away from the engine, pulled the revolver from my pocket, thumbed back the safety, and lined it up. I had to wrap my left arm about the railing to keep my footing.

The Albatross came on. Kemal opened up, and I saw chips of wood and glass erupt from the gondola as his bullets hit home. I gasped; somehow, it was worse to see the machine-gun inflict the damage than to endure it.

"O Lord," I prayed, "protect Ari from those bullets." After a pause, I added, "And Sikorsky too, and Fr. Jamie, and Fritz. Amen."

I squeezed the trigger.

Nothing happened.

With dismay, I realized I had forgotten to reload my revolver down in the wheel-house.

I looked up from the gun to the aeroplane. Kemal had seen me, and he was swinging the muzzle of the machine-gun upwards. Fire flashed from the muzzle.

I hit the floor of the gantry, a grunt escaping from my lips. At the same moment, I heard bullets impact on the envelope over my head. One loud *ding* told me one had hit the engine directly. I started to curse, but my grumbling turned to a yell of fear and surprise: I had begun to slide along the gantry, for it sloped away below me. The Albatross sped away along the port-side of the airship, and Fr. Jamie and Fritz opened up as it passed. Then it was gone.

But I had a different problem now: I was sliding fast down the gantry. I reached out to catch hold of the guard-rail, but I was going too fast. Below me, the barrier at the end was a mere two rods of steel with wide spaces between—ample room for me to fall through. And we were still two hundred feet above the reservoir. "*He-e-elp!*" I cried, though I could hardly tell to whom. My fingers opened, and my gun flew out into the air. I reached out, and felt my hand repeatedly striking the upright supports of the gantry rail.

My slippery journey stopped when I hit the gantry end-rail. I fell forward, and the steel rods struck me across the stomach. My legs swung, and I could feel that horrible sensation of my stomach flying out way below me. Grunting like a beast, I scrabbled to catch hold of something—anything. My mouth was dry, my fingers slippery with sweat, and I could feel the steel rods slipping between them. I slid a little further, my heart pounding in my ears, and my legs flew out and into space. Below me, I could see the glittering surface of the reservoir, but I knew it would feel like hitting concrete from this height.

I still had one arm free and, with it, I flailed around, trying to get a better grip. Each time, I slipped further down, and I had begun to despair when, finally, I was able to close my fingers about the gantry and pull.

But there was no budging me for the moment. I was far too heavy, and for an uncharitable moment I cursed Fritz's cooking.

The Albatross was back—I could hear the Mercedes engine growing steadily in volume over the roar of the air and our own engines. I stole a glance over my shoulder. There was Kemal in the back seat, the gun a hollow black dot as it lined up on me. I wanted to close my eyes, to turn away from the flying death; but I couldn't tear my eyes from it.

But before Kemal could open fire, the Albatross shuddered and sank away from us. It turned over slowly, then turned over again, all the time rapidly losing altitude. When it hit the ground, it was the right way up, but the wrong angle. The undercarriage shattered, and its starboard wings hit a tree. They crumpled at once, and the plane came to a halt. It didn't explode. That only happens in books.

I was still hanging over the gantry, my legs dangling in space. I relaxed a moment, offered up a silent prayer of thanks, then hauled myself back onto the gantry. In a moment, I was sprawled on the steel deck, and I struggled back to the Number 3 engine. Alas, I could see it would take a couple of hours of work—there was no patching it. And my tools had gone over the side long ago. I hurried back through the maintenance hatch and into the wheel-house. Everybody was there.

"It was a superb shot, Fritz," said Fr. Jamie, slapping the little German on the back.

"*Danke, Vater,*" replied Fritz.

"Everybody to hold on!" called Sikorsky. "Landing will be rough." He looked inquiringly at me, but I shook my head.

The LS3 leaned over to port, and land appeared—mostly flat land, but scattered with trees. Our descent was not fast, so there did not seem to be any danger, but Sikorsky was frustrated at not being able to control it. Steadily, we lost altitude, while he muttered and fumed in Russian.

"Pardon my language," he said, after a moment.

"That's okay," I said. "I don't understand Russian."

"I do," said Ari. "You should be ashamed of yourself, Vasili Ivanovich."

Sikorsky blushed.

"Did you kill him, Fritz?" asked Ari.

Fritz looked almost offended. "Frau McCracken," he said, "I aim for his hand, and I get his hand. He cannot fly without his hand. But the plane, it crash—I see it all. Maybe he no longer lives now."

"Please to hold on tight!" shouted Sikorsky, and we all grabbed what stable objects we could.

The airship lurched, and the branches of a tree thrust themselves through the windows beside me. The LS3 rotated slowly about the tree, sagged over to the starboard side, and dropped. It rattled from side to side, and then came at last to rest.

We had crash-landed in Zun.

CHAPTER 10
THE LAND OF ZUN

The LS3 came to rest, canted slightly to the starboard, but more or less level other than that. The landing had tossed us around a bit, and we picked ourselves up, shaken, a little bruised, certainly bewildered. Out of the starboard windows, through the jagged spikes of broken glass, we could see grass sloping down to the vivid blue of the reservoir. Trees, mostly dark pines interspersed with birches, gold and crimson now for the autumn, blanketed the slope. Out of the port windows, the ground ascended through thickly growing pines towards unseen heights.

"Let's take a wee peek at this, shall we!" cried Fr. Jamie, heading for the door. Ari and Fritz went with him, but Sikorsky and I exchanged glances.

"Let's take a wee peek at the damage," I suggested. Sikorsky nodded and we went together up the steps to the upper deck, and from there through a trapdoor into the envelope. We paused to put on felt shoes, which wouldn't spark on the steel gantries and cause an explosion.

It was dark when we first entered but Sikorsky indicated shafts of lights like spears criss-crossing the huge space.

"Bullet holes," I concluded.

"*Da*," agreed Sikorsky. He threw a switch and, with a fizz and an electric hum, the dozens of halogen floodlights flickered on. The huge, cavernous space was revealed by the garish white light. It was four hundred feet long, filled mostly with the three spherical ballonets that contained the hydrogen. Gantries led along the airship's equator and spanned the gap from side to side. It was from these that we could perform routine maintenance or more extensive repairs.

Sikorsky spat out a couple of harsh words in Russian. I didn't have to ask him for a translation. The middle ballonet sagged a little towards the top, and the sides were just slightly hollowed. Its Euclidean perfection was compromised. It couldn't deflate entirely, as it was secured to the envelope supports with massive braces of steel, but it was as empty of hydrogen as a hydrogen ballonet could possibly be.

"Is much damage!" lamented Sikorsky. "Will take many time to repair." His grammar always suffered when he was distressed.

"Do we have enough spare hydrogen?" I asked.

"If those brutes have not shot the spare canisters, *da*." We walked along the deck at the bottom of the envelope to where ranks upon ranks of compressed gas canisters stood on steel racks, held secure by canvas belts. "We have much hydrogen," Sikorsky said, "but repairs to ballonet take much time. First, I must find holes. Then I patch each one. Many tests I will run. Ballonet must be completely air-tight, or it will not lift dirigible."

"Well, once again the Sons of Martha will have to take care of it," I said. "Shall we go and tell the Children of Mary?"

Sikorsky nodded and threw the switch that plunged the envelope again into darkness. A few moments later, we stepped through the door of the gondola and onto the ground. It was strange that the gondola was resting upon the ground, and that we used neither rope-ladder nor mobile steps to descend. Sikorsky and I ran our eyes up and down the airship.

"Is good it was middle ballonet hit," said Sikorsky, pointing fore and aft.

That had been fortunate, I reflected. If the aft ballonet had been hit, the airship would have sagged astern, and that would have wrecked the tail; if the forward ballonet had been deflated, the same thing would have happened to its nose.

But Sikorsky was still grieving over the hit. "Is big mess." He shook his head sadly. "Aiyee! What would I give for my workshop in Kiev now! Why must I suffer like this?"

"Careful," I warned him, "you're beginning to sound like a character in a Dostoevsky novel."

I caught Sikorsky's eye, and he flashed a grin at me. "I know," he said. "I shut up now."

"Still," I went on, looking around, "it doesn't look like we'll find much of what we want around here."

We were in fact in a most pleasant spot. Overhead was a yellow and crimson canopy, birch-like trees in their first blush of autumn. The ground sloped up to snow-capped mountains above us, but pines gathered in a thick forest almost as far as the very top. I could see what looked like an aspen stand, like a spilling of gold coins amid the dark green, towards the tree-line. But there was no sign of habitation. I looked in the other direction.

Sikorsky had read my thoughts. "Perhaps we seek down by lake," he suggested, and we trudged around the gondola, our feet crunching on the first leaf-fall, and down the slope towards the water.

That was where we found the others, staring about themselves in solemn wonder. Through the trees, we could see a flash of gold and blue, where the sun struck the waters of the reservoir; beyond it, the further bank was lined with a pale beach, above which pine forests reached up to the snowy peaks of the far side of the valley.

Ari turned to me as Sikorsky and I approached. "This is one of the most beautiful places I've ever seen," she said quietly.

Together, we strolled down through the slender trees towards the water. We came to a place where the ground dropped away steeply, and below us, we could see how the trees marched down almost to the shore.

"When I was a kid," said Ari, "my Uncle Teddy used to take me to places like this. One of my favourites was a place he called Glacier National Park. It looked a lot like this."

"Uncle Teddy?"

"He wasn't my real uncle," she replied evasively. "Just a friend of the family. But he was like an uncle to me."

The reservoir, I saw now, was wide, and on it we observed a number of boats. Most of them had spread no sail, but nets were thrown over the side. They bobbed up and down gently on the little waves. There was no sound save the soft sighing of the wind in the trees.

Far off to our right, the pale line of the dam stretched across the furthest end of the reservoir. We had come quite a way during our battle with Kemal and the Albatross.

"Now, that's beautiful," I said. "I wonder what it's made from? When we looked at it from the other side, we were too far away to see any details. I wish I could get a closer look. How old do you think it is?"

"Look!" cried Ari. "An osprey!"

"I mean, the oldest dam in the world is almost five thousand years old," I went on, "the Jawa Dam in Jordan. It's a fantastic feat of engineering! You have to have technology or a huge workforce to build a dam."

Ari was turning about on her heel. "This is such a fertile place," she said in wonderment. "Look at all the growth—the trees, the bushes, the flowers, and the fields we saw on the way in. Yet all around it are deserts!"

"Do you think we could get to it before night-fall?" I wondered. "How thick do you think it is?"

"How thick what is?" Ari's lips were twisted, and she stared at me with incomprehension.

"The dam, of course," I said irritably. "What else could I be talking about?" I took a few steps for-ward. "I wonder if it's an arch-dam or a gravity-dam?"

"What are you talking about?" wondered Ari.

I turned in exasperation back to her. "An arch-dam," I said, "is one that has a flat face towards the water, and gains its stability from arches on the landward side. See?" She didn't. "A gravity-dam is solid, and uses the weight of the dam itself to push against the force of the water."

"Perhaps they can tell us." Ari pointed. A small group of people, about eight in all, were striding up the slope towards us, way off to our right. It was hard to get a proper look at them through the trees, but the men seemed to wear mostly dark-coloured tunics that came down to their knees, the women brighter colours, long and flowing scarlets and greens, with floral patterns embroidered in gold. All of them, men and women, wore fur caps. The men were all bearded, and some of the whiter beards were very long indeed.

I turned at a noise behind us, and saw that the others, Sikorsky and Fr. Jamie and Fritz, were scrambling down the incline towards us, their eyes on the newcomers.

Those newcomers had now halted and stood looking at us for a long moment, speckled with sunlight that came through the trees above. I think we must have been expecting them to make a move, but they just stared at us, slack-jawed. One of them whispered to another, and pointed. I followed her finger, and saw that she was pointing at the LS3.

"They do not seem to want to kill us," observed Sikorsky.

"But what *do* they want?" I wondered.

"Let's see if I can figure anything out," said Ari, in a tone of voice that suggested rolling up her sleeves. She took a few paces to the front.

Seeing her move, the oldest of the men stepped forward, and holding out his empty hands, spoke a few words.

Ari snatched a glance back at me. "It sounds a little like some old form of Turkish," she said. "Almost."

She turned back to the Zunians and spoke a few halting phrases. They looked at each other, chattering and pointing at Ari. She shrugged. "That was Turkish," she explained. "They don't seem to understand. It's strange, though—some of their words sound Greek, and some are something else."

"Aramaic," said Fr. Jamie firmly.

Ari's eyebrows shot up, and I asked, "How can you tell?"

"Och, lad, I took two years of Aramaic in seminary," answered Fr. Jamie. "I canna understand mickle when it's spoken, but I ken a few words. That one there—" he pointed as surreptitiously as he could at the elder with the white beard leading them, "said *Yahweh*."

"Yahweh!" I cried. "God?" And even as I said it, one of them solemnly made the sign of the cross—backwards, true, and finishing on the left shoulder, but clear and unmistakable.

"Let's try this," said Fr. Jamie with determination. He strode forward, dropped to his knees, and declared in a loud voice: "*Aboon dabashmaya, nethkadash shamak, tetha mal-koothak!*"

"What's he doing?" I asked Ari out of the side of my mouth.

"Praying the Our Father in Aramaic," she replied.

The effect on the Zunians was immediate and striking. They all cried out for joy and fell to their knees, joining in with Fr. Jamie's prayer. He finished, crossed himself, and got to his feet, the Zunians crowding him and thumping him on the back, shaking his hand, reaching up to kiss him on the cheek—they were mostly shorter than he.

Fr. Jamie looked over his shoulder at us. "The Land of Zun was evangelized by St. Thomas the Apostle—Doubting Thomas," he said with glee. "He would have spoken Aramaic."

"They weren't speaking Aramaic earlier," Ari pointed out.

"Nay," answered Fr. Jamie, "and we don't speak Latin to each other every day, but it's the language of the liturgy—we hear it at Mass every Sunday." He beamed. "I just spoke to them in the language of Our Lord Himself!" he exclaimed.

"Well done," I said.

"Thanks be to God," he replied.

One of the women stepped forward. She pointed to the LS3, then up into the sky, talking slowly as she did so. Then she mimed a bird flying, then pointed downwards. Ari nodded vigorously, and tried to repeat the phrases the woman had used. The woman laughed, and repeated her words. Ari said it again and again, until she got it right. Turning to me, smiling, she said, "Well, now I know how to say, 'We flew here in a bird-ship and crashed into a tree' in Zunian."

"I expect that'll be useful," I remarked.

The old man started talking to Ari, slowly and deliberately. When he had finished, he repeated himself. Ari replied, and the old man repeated himself again. Again, Ari spoke, until Sikorsky asked, "What is happen?"

Ari explained, "I think they want to take us to a place called Bashkent."

"The Holy City of Bashkent!" declared Fr. Jamie. "It's mentioned in the manuscript, so it is!"

Ari nodded. "It seems to be their capital city, south of here, I think. I can't tell how far—several days' journey, maybe."

But Sikorsky shook his head. "Here I must stay," he said, "to repair LS3."

"Poor Vasili!" lamented Ari, putting a hand on his shoulder. "Repairing her seems to be your whole life!"

"Is not so bad," answered Sikorsky, shrugging. "She is good old lady." Looking at me, he added, "I don't want to sound like character in Dostoevsky novel."

Ari turned back to the old man and asked him a question, miming as she spoke. The old man replied likewise. They had to speak to each other several times before Ari turned back to us, saying, "He wants us all to go and meet someone."

"Who?" asked Fr. Jamie.

"Someone he calls Prester Khan," answered Ari.

"Prester Khan?" repeated Fr. Jamie, his head snapping back towards her in surprise. "Not Prester John?"

"Prester Khan," confirmed Ari. "I asked him especially on that. Apparently, Prester John was a mistake. Remember, it's spelt *Cuan* in the manuscript. I thought it was just a way of representing a heavily aspirated initial consonant, like Juan in Spanish, but I'd guess Prester Khan is actually a title, not a name."

"Priest-king," said Fr. Jamie. "That makes sense. Then Prester Khan was never one man—he was a succession of men, priest-kings of Zun."

The woman who had mimed for Ari earlier started doing it again, and for a few minutes, she and Ari talked and mimed and waved their arms about. In the end, Ari said, "They're inviting us to stay with them this evening—they are all family members, and they live on the edge of the reservoir, making their living by fishing. The old man's name is Peisko. We need to see Prester Khan, but we can begin the journey tomorrow morning. Peisko will guide us."

"Tell them we accept!" said Fr. Jamie with enthusiasm. "I'll get my Mass kit." And he dashed off to retrieve it from his cabin.

The Zunians led us down the slope, through terraced fields now in stubble, towards their tiny collection of cottages with thatched roofs that were clustered about a central courtyard next to the shore. A number of boats were drawn up on a wide beach, painted mostly black and red, and dismasted for the evening, their sails folded neatly. Further along the shore, we could see other such tiny communities, hiding among the foliage that came down right to the beach.

All the time, the Zunians watched us closely, and made excited whispers behind their hands when they thought we weren't looking.

They led us to one of the little houses. Judging by the lichen growing in the cracks between the stones, it was an old building, several centuries at least, the thatch dark grey above. I remembered hearing once that some of the thatched roofs in England were centuries old—this one looked it.

Peisko pulled open the door, and we descended three steps to get to a neatly-swept floor. The ceiling was low, and in the far corner, over some counters and a wood stove, nets of turnips hung from stout, dark rafters. In the nearer part of the room was a long table, about which were arranged wooden chairs. The walls were whitewashed, the windows and doorway picked out in red brick. Some steps to our left led up to another story, others down into a cellar.

Over the fireplace (which Peisko hurried to light) was a crucifix. Fr. Jamie virtually did a pirouette on seeing it. "A Christian land amidst the Moslems!" he chanted in delight. He peered closely at it. "Look how the figure's just about jumping off the cross, and how wide His blessed wounds are!" he enthused.

One of the women fetched some food—fish, bread, fresh vegetables, with some dark red wine to complement it.

But then came a rattle at the door, and a voice cried out to us within. The old man opened the door, concern on his face, and admitted a group of younger men carrying what looked like a stretcher.

On it, his eyes squeezed shut and his face grey with pain, was Kemal.

CHAPTER 11
THE LONG LAKE

A couple of men pushed the table on which we had been eating out of the way, and they set Kemal down on the floor. Ari and Fritz knelt beside him and conducted a quick examination.

"His leg's broken," said Ari. "Some lacerations, some bruising, but otherwise he'll be okay."

Hearing her voice, Kemal opened his eyes wide in horror. "I will not be tended by a woman!" he hissed.

I could see that Kemal was on the point of getting a tongue-lashing, but Fr. Jamie gently placed his hand on Ari's shoulder. He shook his head, almost imperceptibly. Ari nodded and stepped away from the wounded man. "Fritz," she said, "you'd better tend him. I'll get the first-aid kit from the LS3."

"*Jawohl, mein Dame,*" replied Fritz, and Ari dashed out of the house. One of the women brought some water, and Fritz set about bathing Kemal's wounds. All the time, Kemal cursed him and all but frothed at the mouth with rage.

"What happened to the pilot?" asked Fr. Jamie.

"He is dead," Kemal said through gritted teeth. "He was killed by the infidel, and now he takes his ease in Jannah."

"They didn't just leave his body there!" Fr. Jamie sounded shocked. But one of the men who had brought Kemal tugged at Fr. Jamie's sleeve and pointed through the window. "Ah," said Fr. Jamie, "the other men have gone back for the pilot's body; they'll bury it before nightfall."

Kemal stopped cursing and cried, "You cannot give him Christian burial! He is upon the path, light shines upon him! You cannot bury him with the rites of the Infidel!"

"Don't worry, Kemal," Fr. Jamie reassured him, "we'll do nothing of the kind. You can pray the *Janazah*, and we'll make sure his grave is aligned towards Mecca. I'm sure he was a faithful follower of the light."

Kemal swallowed, and fell silent for a few seconds. "He was my brother," he said at last.

The awkward silence was broken by Ari's return with the first-aid kit, and Fritz busied himself bandaging Kemal's wounds and binding his broken leg in a splint. That set him off again, and he indulged once more in cursing and snarling.

We left the following morning, an hour or so after the sun rose in the cleft between two snowy peaks across the lake. Peisko and a couple of his sons, themselves in their late fifties, prepared one of the boats and we all boarded, carefully carrying the bitterly complaining Kemal in and setting him down in the bottom of the boat. Sikorsky stayed on the shore, with Fritz.

"McCracken," said Sikorsky, "we will repair what we can of LS3."

"*Auf weidersehen, Herr McCracken und Frau McCracken*," called Fritz. "Return soon, *bitte!*"

Peisko cast off, then unfurled the sail. The wind tugged at it gently and the prow clove through the waters, sending up a little foam, the triangular bow-wave spreading behind us like a fan. I looked at the lines of the ship, noting its deep draught and wide beam—she was made for storing large quantities of fish, not for speed.

The voyage was never dull, for the land we sailed through was incomparably beautiful: snow-capped mountains rose on either side, deep forests or lush fields covering the foothills. We saw no towns or cities, but there were many homesteads sprinkled throughout.

"Ariadne, my dear," said Fr. Jamie, "would you be so kind as to ask our guide where the cities of Zun are?"

After a few moments exchanging words with Peisko, Ari replied, "There is a city, Bashkent, where we are going. But it seems there are no other cities."

"Are there local lords, or landowners of any kind?" asked Fr. Jamie.

After a few moments, Ari answered, "He doesn't seem to understand the question. Everyone owns his own land. There is Prester Khan, who lives in Bashkent. There is no one else; he is their lord under God."

"Fascinating," said Fr. Jamie. "Every man is the master of his own plot of ground."

"Isn't that true everywhere?" I asked.

"In a way," answered Fr. Jamie. "In most countries of Europe, men have to work for large corporations—the governments, the banks, the factories. Here, they seem to work for themselves. They're truly independent. Do you remember the encyclical our Holy Father Leo wrote last century, *Rerum Novarum*?" I shook my head. "Och, laddie, your education's been sadly lacking these last few years, so it has. The Holy Father Leo was talking about justice and economics. The idea that governments should have any control over families and households at all he called 'a great and pernicious error.' He did, it's as true as I'm sitting here in this boat with the two of you. Every family should grow its own food, make its own goods to sell, educate its own children, if it can. Everyone should be in charge of his own wealth. No one should be dependent on a government or a large corporation. That's Catholic economics and justice, but of course it's never been realized in the West, except on a small scale. Here, everyone seems to practice it."

There was silence for a moment, then Ari said, "Things are still like that back home. In America, there are men who still own family homesteads, especially on the frontiers."

"Aye, but how long will that last? Even now, the corporations are growing bigger. Without the Faith, lass, even America is doomed."

The boat ploughed on through the water for a few moments, bobbing as it struck a wave. I said, "There are no lords here except Prester Khan. But didn't the manuscript say that Pero da Covilha was Duke of somewhere?"

"Aye, Guzelvadi," replied Fr. Jamie. "Another mystery I hope will be solved when we meet Prester Khan."

Shortly after this, Peisko pulled on the tiller and brought the boat in to land. And there, in a wide coombe leading up from the lake shore, was a large house belonging to the sons of his cousin. We carried Kemal, who regarded us with a baleful eye but said nothing, out of the boat, dismasted it, and dragged it a little way up the beach.

A voice rang out from the top of the beach, and we all looked up to see that a collection of men had arrived. They all looked like Peisko, some of an age with him, some much younger. They were armed with swords and staves, and a couple of them carried torches that cast a pool of golden light around them.

Ari and I braced ourselves for a confrontation; I fingered the hilt of my revolver.

But then Peisko called out, and advanced rapidly up the beach towards them, his arms wide. On seeing Peisko, the newcomers cried out for surprise and joy and embraced him, chattering confusingly in their strange language. Ari and I looked at one another and followed Peisko up the beach.

"Peisko's family, I presume," I said.

"It looks like it."

Peisko turned and indicated us, pointing to the sky frequently. They all regarded us with wonder—almost with awe—then advanced upon us and embraced each one of us in turn.

"Why do they keep doing that?" I asked Ari in an aside. "Why do they keep pointing to the sky and looking at us *like that*?"

Ari shrugged. "I guess they just don't have flight yet," she suggested.

"Hardly surprising," commented Fr. Jamie. "How long is it since the Wright Brothers? Ten years? Flight's relatively new, even for us. Here—well, if it comes at all, it may be decades or even centuries in the future."

A couple of Peisko's relatives picked up Kemal's stretcher, and they led us away from the beach and along a path. There were thick bushes, darkened now by the falling night, on either side, and the forest loomed up beyond them.

"You know, flying could really help them a lot here," I said. "They could reach different parts of Zun much more swiftly. And the principles of aerodynamics are relatively simple—I could teach them everything they would need to know. Ari, ask them if they'd like my help in building aeroplanes."

"I dinna think they'll be wanting that, Cracky," said Fr. Jamie.

"Why not?" I asked; but Fr. Jamie just shrugged while Ari conveyed my question. There was silence for a few moments, and then she said in response to their words, "They say thank you, Mac, but they don't think they'll need to fly like birds."

"Told you," said Fr. Jamie with a quick smile.

But before I could respond, there was a low, throaty growl from the shadows at the side of the road ahead of us. The LS3 crew looked quickly at each other, puzzlement in our eyes. Slowly, Peisko's relatives lowered Kemal to the ground; I drew my revolver and thumbed back the safety.

The Zunians tensed and gathered together, drawing their swords and knives, one of them lowering his stave.

Kemal looked left and right, raising himself on one elbow. "What happens?" he demanded.

I knelt down beside him and whispered, "It sounds like a large cat of some kind."

Even as I spoke, the cat emerged from the shadows. The torchlight shone across its flank, and I swear it was scarlet, like rust. It was a little smaller than a male lion, and it had no mane. Its green eyes glowed in the gloaming. I could smell its cat-musk, and my nose wrinkled. Rising slowly, I leveled my revolver at it. It snarled at us. Carefully taking aim—I could hardly miss at this range—I squeezed the trigger.

The hammer fell with a hollow click. My revolver had misfired.

The lion's eyes snapped on me, and it glowered with ill temper. The Zunians tensed, their weapons raised. One of them held his torch out towards the lion. It growled again, then looked at each of us in turn, and slunk off into the forest.

A sigh of relief rippled through the Zunians. They started chattering animatedly with each other and laughing. I fumbled with my revolver, snapping open the chamber to see what had gone wrong with it. I emptied the ammunition and dropped it into my pocket, snapping the chamber back into place and cocking the hammer. Sure enough, the firing pin was broken. I needed to work on it back on the LS3—something highly unlikely, given that the airship was now a day's journey behind us. In the meantime, the weapon was useless. Muttering curses to myself, I slid it back into the holster and buttoned the flap over it.

Ari said, "These red lions are common in the mountains, they say. But when winter begins to close in, they come down to the plains looking for food. This is not uncommon."

"But this is," I said, slapping my revolver.

"I'm sorry your toy didn't work," said Ari, slipping her arm in mine and kissing me on the cheek, "but you're not on safari now. And I think the stick with the fire on it worked pretty well, don't you?"

I grumbled a little, and we started out again along the path.

Peisko's family lived in a large house from which you could just see the lake. Wide fields lay on either side of it and, beyond them, the forest stretched up over the foothills. Peisko explained to us that the forest-people lived there—they hunted wild boar and deer and traded meat and skins with the homesteaders and at the markets in Bashkent. They also traded bone tools of all kinds—knives, mostly, but also spoons and needles, awls and fishhooks, rings, bracelets, beads, and tiny statues of the beasts they hunted. Further up, in the high mountain pastures, the herders tended their flocks of sheep and goats. Peisko's family got milk and wool from them, and some meat. Right now, the herders were bringing their flocks down into the lower pastures for winter.

The house sprawled—a number of out-buildings stood around a central lodge that rose two stories above the rest. The ground floor of the main building comprised a single wide and tall room, a hall in which the family gathered, the kitchen, and the food storage areas. On the top floors were the private rooms in which they slept. We were lodged in one of the out-buildings, though Peisko took a room in the house itself.

Peisko's family treated us like royalty, laying before us roast lamb, couscous, and a variety of vegetables, some of which I didn't recognize. After the meal, the Zunians brought out musical instruments—something that looked like a strange violin, but was called a *ghijak*, some pipes, and tambourines—and we danced for hours, as tired as we were after our trip.

At least, Fr. Jamie and Ari danced. I've never been much of a dancer myself. But at the height of the festivities, a little girl of about six years with jet-black hair bound up in a red ribbon, wearing a pretty scarlet dress, pulled me out onto the dance floor. By gestures and urgent words I couldn't understand, she got me to imitate the other dancers. When she was sure I had got the dance-steps, she led me, still dancing, across the floor to Ari and made me dance with her. From then on, I occasionally caught a glimpse of her, looking at me appraisingly from between a couple of adults at the edge of the dance floor.

Some of the dances were wild, like fires along the hillsides; others were slow and highly formal, and it was mainly the women who danced for the men at this point, their arms outstretched, their heads motionless as they dipped first to the left, and then to the right.

But the hall seemed very warm and stuffy to me, so I threw on my jacket and climbed the stairs to the balcony, from where I knew I could see the lake, stretched out silver in the moonlight below us. Fr. Jamie was there ahead of me, his breath steaming in the night, gazing at the lake.

"Good evening, Cracky," he said, as I approached.

For a while, we contemplated the scene in silence, and listened to the strange music from downstairs. It seemed almost as if the music emanated from the hills, from the trees, from the lake itself.

At last, I broke the silence by remarking, "It's hard to believe that, right now, there are boys shooting at one another from trenches in Belgium and France."

"This is the way God meant us to live, Cracky," said Fr. Jamie quietly, nodding to the courtyard, the little out-buildings, and the lake beyond. "He didn't mean for us to live in cities, to work in factories. He made the land for us. Whenever we make something for ourselves, we mess it up."

"The house was made by men, not by God," I pointed out.

"Aye," replied Fr. Jamie, "but it was made to suit the land. Look at a city back home—look at Birmingham, or Wolverhampton. Why should they even exist? They're offenses to every sense God gave men—they're eyesores, they stink, they're filthy beyond belief."

"They can be improved," I suggested.

"Perhaps," agreed Fr. Jamie. "It's possible they might be cleaned up by some future generations and made into decent places to live. But they'll still be cities. The folks living in one street will never eat at the house of folk living in the next street, nor say 'Good day' to the man they pass on the High Street. The problem, I think, is the size. Look at this." He gestured to the thatched roofs on the out-buildings. "These houses look like people. The thatch is like their hair, the walls like their bodies. The out-buildings are like limbs." He smiled, because I suppose I was looking a little doubtful at his rhapsody. "Aye, mock if you like," he said. "But this is natural. Our cities back in England and Scotland are not."

Something of a fear came over me. "Are you thinking you might want to stay here?" I asked.

"Och no," he answered rapidly. "I'd sore like to, mind—my heart is full here. But I ken that fullness like this is only a mockery this side of Paradise. And I'm nay my own man. I'm God's missionary, and I must ever live in mission territory." He breathed the night air in deeply, and I could smell the damp pines all around. "But this," he concluded, "this is a little slice of the Kingdom. At least, now, I know what I'm guiding folk towards."

We slept late the next day, and sailed no further until the sun had set and risen one more time. Then, once more, the boat slid through the dark waters of the lake, the trees on either side of us gold and russet, the skies vivid and blue. No one said anything, but sat there in the sternsheets or, in Fr. Jamie's case, in the bows, staring in wonder at the land unfolding around us. Even Kemal stopped complaining.

The sun was low over the western mountaintops when something dark appeared on the lake ahead of us. Soon, it resolved into a small city, sitting on great wooden piles in the middle of the lake. The roofs, some of copper and some of red tiles, rose from stone walls, and the dying sunlight flashed on thousands of glazed windows.

Peisko spoke a few words to Ari, who relayed them to us. "That's Bashkent," she said. "It's the royal city of Prester Khan."

CHAPTER 12
THE ROYAL CITY OF THE PRIEST-KING

Peisko moored the little vessel among the forest of piers below the city, and we climbed wooden steps to the street level. Ari and I carried the stretcher, while Fr. Jamie slung Kemal over his shoulders. The ascent was like moving from one world to another: below, all was wood and water; at street level, all was stone. Some of the houses were plastered and painted in flaking reds, blues, and yellows. Some sported murals of famous inhabitants of Zun or episodes from Zunian history, or just a sunrise or mountain-scape. On the upper stories were balconies, where people sat and conversed, sometimes leaning out over the street to talk to neighbours across the way; sometimes they played games that looked like chess or backgammon.

Shadows lay dark across the street, but still they thronged with brightly-clad people. Kemal, back on his stretcher by now, attracted some curiosity. Some of Bashkent's inhabitants offered Peisko a cheerful greeting as we passed, and some of them stopped to converse. This led, as usual, to gestures towards the sky, the pointing of fingers at us, and the appearance of awe and sometimes even fear upon the faces of those who had not yet heard that we had flown into Zun like birds.

"Peisko seems to know a lot of people," I remarked.

"Aye," agreed Fr. Jamie. "I wonder how many folk I'd stop to chat with on the Royal Mile in Edinburgh."

"I wouldn't even want to talk to the people I met in New York," added Ari.

At length, we reached a wide cobbled square in the centre of the city. At the far end were two buildings. On the left stood a church built in an eastern fashion, with domes like huge cloves of garlic. Next to it was the royal palace, a three-story building with an arched colonnade stretching the whole length of the front. It was painted white, with red chevrons running in horizontal lines across it, broken only by the windows and balconies of the upper stories.

Inside, Peisko spoke to a guard, with all the usual gesticulations, while we set Kemal down on the polished marble floor. The guard looked something like a Swiss Guard, with brightly-coloured, slashed sleeves, white hose and shining breastplate. His eyes widened on hearing Peisko's story. He stared at us for a moment, then fled up the stairs.

"I'm not sure I like that response," I commented.

Ari, who had joined Peisko, listened to him a few moments, spoke a couple of times, then turned and said, "The guard has gone to see if he can get an audience with Prester Khan."

"Look at this, Cracky," urged Fr. Jamie, indicating one of the walls, which was covered with paintings. "It's a visual history of Zun. I think this must be St. Thomas." There was indeed a picture of St. Thomas, searching the wounds of Our Lord. But other pictures showed various people at work, ploughing fields or milking cows, herding sheep or hunting in the dense forests, throwing pots on wheels or hammering iron. Some paintings were portraits of impressive Zunians, both men and women, some of the men perhaps previous Prester Khans. There were pictures of local animals, including one of a bright red lion, such as the one we had confronted two nights ago. All the paintings were accomplished in a style that reminded me a little of Byzantine icons, a little of illustrations from the *Arabian Nights*.

"Please please," said Peisko, hurrying up to us—so much English he had learned from Ari. He was gesturing towards the wide stairs, where the guard waited, his eyes still wide, like friction wheels. Fr. Jamie and I each took one end of Kemal's stretcher and followed Peisko and the guard up the stairs. Peisko had removed his cap and fumbled with it nervously as we ascended.

"This is splendid," observed Fr. Jamie of the paintings and the magnificent architecture. "It's like

Blenheim, or the Hofburg in Vienna." I grunted in reply—I had to hold Kemal higher than Fr. Jamie, as I had the lower end of the stretcher. "All the legends say Prester John was fabulously rich," Fr. Jamie went on. "Seventy kings supposedly served him at his banquets—even allowing for the usual medieval hyperbole, that suggests considerable wealth."

"How can you—talk—when we're—carrying heavy things—up stairs," I huffed, behind him.

"Hmph," replied Fr. Jamie. "I don't think poor Kemal's as heavy as you're implying, Cracky. Talk about medieval hyperbole!"

We had reached the top of the stairs, and for a moment set Kemal down. He snarled upon being set down—I had put my end down a bit roughly.

"Please please," repeated Peisko. He and the guard stood by a pair of wide doors of highly polished oak. The guard's hand was on one gold handle.

"Are you ready, Cracky?" asked Fr. Jamie. "Or would you prefer me to carry this jolly bloke all by myself?"

"The jolly bloke can walk!" snarled Kemal, and he struggled to get off his stretcher. With much hissing and gritting of his teeth, he elevated himself until he was leaning against the balcony rail. But he couldn't move away from it.

Seeing what was happening, Peisko hurried up and offered Kemal his walking-stick. The sullen

Turk took it without a word, and at last the guard opened the doors.

We passed through the doors and entered a throne room. It was wide and airy, with a red domed ceiling covered with intricate designs in gold leaf. Windows on either side let in fresh air and flooded the space with blue light from outside, so that we could see the marble floor, the deep red carpet leading to the dais, the single throne in the middle of the dais.

And upon the throne sat Prester Khan.

He was surrounded by his advisors, mostly bearded and wearing robes of black. He himself wore white, with a faint bluish tinge—the fabric we had come so far to find. He was an older man, though I couldn't estimate an exact age, and he wore a long, white beard below a wizened face from which shone dark, intelligent eyes. On his head stood a tall, flat-topped hat, encircled by a modest band of gold. A cloak of white furs hung about his shoulders.

Peisko dropped to his knees, bowing before Prester Khan, the sole lord of Zun, and we all followed suit—except Kemal, who leaned heavily upon the stick Peisko had lent him. Seeing what we did, he bobbed his head briefly. The guard who had showed us in brought a chair, and Kemal lowered himself into it.

The priest-king of Zun made a gentle, almost loving motion to indicate that we should rise, then beckoned us closer, speaking to Peisko. Peisko replied, pointing up, or at us, or sometimes back along the lake we had sailed to get here.

Suddenly, Peisko was interrupted by a stream of angry words, and we all spun round towards Kemal, who was leaning forward in his chair and yelling in Turkish at Prester Khan.

"What's he saying?" I asked.

"A lot of nonsense," answered Ari. "There's a Turkish army coming, everyone in the valley of Zun will fatten the vultures—that sort of thing."

Kemal's words petered out. There was silence for a moment, and we could hear faint sounds of life from outside the palace—the voices of ordinary people living their ordinary lives in Bashkent. I wondered what Prester Khan would do. He was the sole absolute ruler of Zun. Would he have Kemal executed there and then? Would he have mercy and merely have him expelled from the throne room?

Prester Khan got to his feet, descended from his throne and, with slow paces, crossed the marble floor to where Kemal fumed in his chair. Kemal tried to rise to meet him, but his stick slipped on the slick marble, and he landed with a thump back in the chair, groaning with pain.

Tenderly, like a father with a beloved but wayward child, Prester Khan opened Kemal's shirt and put his hands inside. Kemal yelled furiously and strained away from his touch, but Prester Khan did not take his hands away. Instead, he explored further, touching Kemal's side, his leg, his shoulder.

At some point during the examination, Kemal stopped screaming, and looked in wonder upon Prester Khan. He spoke in Turkish. Prester Khan replied in Zunian, touching his finger to his lips, and made the sign of the cross—backwards, to our eyes—over Kemal's forehead. Then he rose and turned to us, speaking quietly and calmly. Ari translated for us. "Prester Khan says that our friend's wounds are whole now."

And Kemal got to his feet, without touching the stick at all. There were no signs of wounds upon him—no gashes, no bruises—and his leg was no longer broken.

Prester Khan shuffled past us, re-mounted the dais, and lowered himself into his throne. Benevolence hung about him like light robes.

"Well," said Fr. Jamie in quiet awe, "who but a disciple of St. Thomas would have learned so well how to search wounds?"

Prester Khan spoke again, and Ari told us that he would see us the next day or the day after. He beckoned to one of his advisors who stepped smartly forward. His face looked European, but he was dressed like a citizen of Bashkent, in a long-skirted tunic of scarlet, with baggy trousers tucked into calf-length boots. He seemed to be in his late sixties, and wore a moustache and grey hair. He held himself as straight as a piston, as if he had at some time been an army officer.

He listened to Prester Khan for a few moments, then turned to us. He descended from the dais, and offered us his hand, saying in perfect English, "I'm awfully glad to meet you all. My name's Ambrose— Sir Neville Ambrose, of the diplomatic service."

"We have an ambassador in Zun!" I cried out in surprise.

Ambrose coloured a little at this. "Not exactly— I took what you might call a leave of absence. We'll discuss it at more length later. In the meantime, it's enough to know that I'm to be your guide and inter- preter for a few days. If you'd like to come with me, I'll take you to the quarters that have been prepared for you. Am I right in assuming that you two are married?" Ari and I nodded. "Jolly good. Well, shall we go?"

We all turned to follow him, but Ambrose stopped Kemal. "If you would be so good," he said, "please stay a moment with the Khan. He'd like to have a word with you—nothing sinister, you under- stand."

The rest of us followed him out of the throne room and through a few corridors into some splen- did apartments. We had a magnificent view down the length of the lake, with Bashkent spread out be- low us, a maze of tiled roofs. Lights were beginning to glow all over, like jewels fallen from the skies.

Crossing to the sideboard, Ambrose took out a green bottle with an almost spherical bottom and a slender, curved neck, and poured four glasses of something yellowish which he handed to us. "This is called *band-alou*," he explained. "It's made from barley—a tolerable substitution for scotch, but hardly a compensation for losing brandy."

It was indeed a little like whisky—somewhat sweeter, and a little rough for my taste, but still very good. We all sat down in wicker chairs on the balcony, while the shadows deepened all around us.

"I'm afraid I've not been in Zun for very long," Ambrose said, "less than two years, as a matter of fact; but the Khan thought I should be your guide because I speak English." He took out a handkerchief and held it to his mouth to smother a cough. "Rather well, in fact."

"It's grand to hear English again," I said. "I was getting tired of hearing everything through an interpreter."

"I've begun to learn the language, of course," replied Ambrose. "I'm close to fluent. I still don't quite understand the jokes, sometimes. And they're frequent. The good humour of Zun is a wonderful antidote to modern European idiocy."

"How did you get to Zun?" inquired Fr. Jamie, leaning forward and gently inhaling the bouquet of the *band-alou*.

"I was attached to the British embassy in Peking," Ambrose explained. "One day, I left the embassy to explore some of the northern regions of China. I was in a pass, and mist descended upon us. When it lifted, I was cut off from my fellow-travelers. I tried to find them, but never did—instead, I ended up here."

"Have you tried to get back?" asked Ari.

Ambrose swilled his *band-alou* and took another sip. "I did, at first. But you know, the funny thing is that I was never really happy at the embassy. I was in the army most of my life—I reached the rank of captain in the 60th Rifles, and took a wound to the head at Laing's Nek. We lost that battle, but we lost it honourably. There doesn't seem much honour in diplomatic work. I used to call it a life of backs—back-stabbing and back-room deals. Would the Chinese really profit from our corrupt ways? Could we profit from theirs? They're every bit as corrupt as we are. So I wasn't entirely disappointed to find myself in Zun, where what a man says he'll do is what he does." He paused again and looked out over the city. By now, night had fallen, and it looked like a whole galaxy below us. He said, "Sometimes, I wonder if my whole stay in Zun hasn't been just a dream, or a figment of my imagination. It's too perfect, in some ways. Every night, when I go to sleep, I wonder if I'll wake up in my bed in the embassy, and I can't sleep for hours."

"Don't you have any family back in Britain?" asked Ari.

Ambrose shook his head. "My wife died five years ago, one of my boys died storming Gyantse Dzong, my other children are grown. I have no ties back there."

"Neville," said Ari, leaning forward, "wherever we go, the Zunians tell the same story about us, how we flew in, and there seems to be a very strong reaction to it. Do you know why?"

Ambrose nodded. "Yes I do," he admitted, "but I don't really think it's my part to tell you about it. The Khan will tell you when he sees you next, I imagine." He rose, draining his glass. "In the meantime, it's getting late, and so I bid you all a good night. Gentlemen, ma'am." He kissed Ari's hand politely. "I shall call on you about ten."

As he left, Kemal entered. He looked as if somebody had just given him a steam engine for his birthday. We all crowded round him.

"What did Prester Khan want with you?"

A look of confusion came over Kemal. He said, a little hesitantly, "It is not easy for me to say. All my life, I have been a follower of Mohammad, the prophet of Allah. All my life, I have thought Joshua bar Joseph was but another prophet."

"Who?" I asked.

"Jesus, son of Joseph," said Fr. Jamie quickly. "Go on, Kemal."

"What the Khan did to me—I could feel God within me, closing up the wounds. And I thought Prester Khan was God. But he told me the truth. He is not God, but the instrument of God." He swallowed and dropped himself into an armchair. "I told him of the army I have led here. Our army has many weapons—rifles, Gatling guns, explosives, cars with guns mounted on them. It will do much damage to Zun. Prester Khan blessed me, as if my sin was but a trifling matter, and I felt God move within me once more." He rubbed his forehead as if he had a headache. "There is much I must think about. The world is very different now."

The next morning, Ambrose took us around the city—Kemal as well. As we emerged from the palace, he pointed out the basilica next to it, and another building that took up the whole side of the square.

"That's what you might call the university," he said. "Bashkent is where the people of all the outlying regions of Zun send their children for education."

"In what?" asked Ari.

"Oh, in useful things," replied Ambrose airily. "It's primarily a seminary, but Zunians can also learn to compose and recite poetry here, and to paint and sculpt, and throw a pot and weave a basket. It's anything a child can't learn directly from its mother or father. But they can't stay in Bashkent after they're finished—they have to go back. No one lives in

151

Bashkent but the courtiers, the teachers, the students, and the people needed to keep things going for them." He made a gesture around the crowds in the square. "That's why you'll see plenty of old birds, like me, and plenty of fledglings, but very few birds in the prime of life. They're all out in Zun, being useful."

We sampled the food, which was very various, consisting of spiced chicken and lamb, fresh vegetables lightly sautéed or roasted, and fluffy bread with thick, aromatic crusts. Through Ambrose's intervention, Ari managed to exchange some of her jewelry for a long, flowing dress such as the local women wore. It was emerald in colour, with wide sleeves, embroidered at the hems with flowers.

As we were returning to the palace, Ari cried out in surprise and called us over. She pointed to the doorpost of a house, on which were carved Zunian letters. "Do you know what that says?" she asked.

"No," said Fr. Jamie and I; but Ambrose said, "Yes—it's the name of the house: *Guzelvadi*."

"Pero da Covilha was Duke of Guzelvadi!" Fr. Jamie cried out.

"Well, *duke* might be putting it a bit strongly," Ambrose said. "*Lord* is perhaps a better translation. It doesn't really say much about him, whoever he was—every man is lord of his own house in Zun."

In the evening, after a splendid dinner, we watched their harvest festival celebration from our balcony—fireworks that put Guy Fawkes to shame, followed by dancing until we all collapsed from weariness.

The next morning, Ambrose called on us before breakfast to tell us that the Khan wished to see us. He led us through the palace's corridors for a few minutes, before ushering us into the Khan's private chambers, where a sumptuous breakfast had been spread, mainly fresh fruits and lamb. Prester Khan prayed a blessing, and we all sat down.

We had eaten a little without conversation, just savouring the rich and simple flavours of the food, when Prester Khan spoke to Ambrose, who said to us, "The Khan has given me permission to tell you this story, which I'm afraid I don't know well, but which I think will explain all. Anyway, here goes.

"According to Zunian epics, many centuries ago, a Zunian army tried to aid the Pope in his attempt to re-claim the Holy Land for the Christians. This would have been about the time of the Second Crusade. But they couldn't reach the Christian armies, because they were unable to cross the River Tigris. Still, the Khan wished to join his brother Christians of Europe, and some years later, another Prester Khan, a visionary and prophet named Unk, tried again to reach Jerusalem. But Unk Khan was intercepted by an army of Mongols, led by a young war-chief called Temujin—we know him better as Genghis Khan. Genghis wiped out the Zunian army, but as he died, Unk made his last prophecy: that the Zunians would never again leave their valley until men came to them from the sky. That would be the sign from God that it was time to leave, and to mingle again with the folks of the world."

"You mean the Zunians have to leave this valley, and it's our fault?" I cried out.

"We're their doom," added Ari bitterly. "I wish I could take back every step that brought us here."

Fr. Jamie got abruptly to his feet and strode across to the window, gazing out over the city of Bashkent, the lake, the mountains, the fields and forests. The sky was a dazzling blue that morning. "This is not our doing," he said at last, "or not all our doing, anyway. Like the Khan here, we're instruments of God's will. No man could have found Zun until airships and aeroplanes were invented. The people of this land were given possession of it only until it became impossible to hide it any longer. And perhaps now is the time when the Zunians can bring something valuable—their way of life—to the world. Think about Baku, Cracky—all those oil derricks belching out smoke into the air. Think about Belgium, and those muddy trenches, where the boys are squatting up to their knees in mud and blood. Perhaps the world needs the Zunians now, more than the Zunians need Zun."

Ambrose added, "There's something personal in this for me. I've been skeptical of the politics and the cultures of Europe all my life. But here, I seem to have found a perfect place—a place that consistently fulfills my moral expectations. I don't want to leave, gentlemen and ma'am. But I consider myself privileged to have seen this land at all. There are millions sweating in the factories of Europe who will never see the sun rise over this fair land." Prester Khan spoke, and he and Ambrose talked for a few moments before Ambrose turned back to us. "The Khan sees this as God's will, the event his people have awaited for centuries. He will give the order to gather food—it is fortunate you should arrive at the time of the harvest—and begin the journey into the world. The Khan asks how we can remain happy, if we do not follow God's will? The very mountains, he says, once a source of joy, will darken and oppress us."

"It's a bitter thing," I said, "to be able to do nothing for the Zunians but aid them in their defeat."

Kemal nodded. "This land is fair—a land of grass and water. But it is not Jannah, or your Christian Heaven. The forces of the world will align against us, and they are strong, like my Turkish army that seeks a way into this land. They will always prevail. But there is Paradise. There *is* a reward for those who are brave, who are strong, and who live in virtue. The people of Zun cannot have the victory over the forces of the world, but they can have the reward in Paradise—Heaven, as you would call it."

Prester Khan spoke again, and Ambrose translated his words for us: "The Khan wishes me to ask you what reason you have for coming to Zun."

"We came to find something," I replied. "Show him the manuscript, Ari."

CHAPTER 13
THE WEAVERS OF ULEK-DHEGUN

Ari took the manuscript out and passed it on to the Khan. He looked on it, and wonder grew in his eyes. For a moment, he looked up at us, then he began to trace the shapes of the letters with his forefinger. He spoke slowly to Ambrose, who told us, "This is a great artifact of the Zunian people, a letter from a Khan of many centuries ago to Pero, Lord of Guzelvadi. This you know, of course. Pero, the Khan says, was strong in wisdom, and came to Zun from a faraway land—the Khan means Portugal, though I'm afraid he doesn't have the word."

"The fabric from which it's made," I said, "could greatly help my people. And it's what the Turkish army coming from the north is after."

Ambrose translated my words; Prester Khan spoke. Ambrose said, "The people of Zun call this fabric *ulek-dhegun*, or lizard-fire. This afternoon, one will guide you to the place it comes from. Until then, the Khan thanks you for your words, but he must begin preparations for his people's departure from the land of their forefathers."

So it was that, a few hours later, we left Bashkent with Ambrose and a guide, crossing a causeway to the lake shore. The lake was fed at the southern end by a narrow river that emerged from a mountain pass, and it was along the shore of this green river that we trekked. Birches grew densely along the banks, rising to thick forests of pine higher up, and the wind rattled through the golden leaves, as if whispering secrets in our ears.

"This pass," Ambrose explained, "leads to China, and it's the way I entered Zun. It will be the way the people of Zun will leave. In a way, you have arrived at just the right moment: the harvest has been gathered, and they will have plenty of food to last them until they find a place to live."

Before long, we came to a collection of wooden huts built on the shore. A mill-wheel turned swiftly in the river's current, and we could hear the stones grinding together inside it. People flooded out of the huts to greet us, the women wiping their hands, the children thronging and singing with merry voices.

"These are the people of Ulek-dhegun," Ambrose told us. "They take the thread and weave it into fabric. Come with me. I want to show you something."

He spoke with one of the men, who nodded and led him away from the people. We followed. On the edge of the little settlement stood a windowless building made of logs. The roof sloped steeply, presumably to slough off snow in the winter-time. The